THE CAT'S PAJAMAS

BY RAY BRADBURY

Ahmed and the Oblivion Machines
Bradbury Stories
The Cat's Pajamas
Dandelion Wine
Dark Carnival
Death Is a Lonely Business
Driving Blind
Fahrenheit 451
From the Dust Returned
The Golden Apples of the Sun
A Graveyard for Lunatics
Green Shadows, White Whale
The Halloween Tree
I Sing the Body Electric!
The Illustrated Man
Let's All Kill Constance
Long After Midnight
The Martian Chronicles
The Machineries of Joy
A Medicine for Melancholy
The October Country
One More for the Road
Quicker Than the Eye
R Is for Rocket
The Stories of Ray Bradbury
S Is for Space
Something Wicked This Way Comes
The Toynbee Convector
When Elephants Last in the Dooryard Bloomed
Witness and Celebrate
Yestermorrow
Zen in the Art of Writing

THE CAT'S PAJAMAS

stories

RAY BRADBURY

WILLIAM MORROW
An Imprint of HarperCollins*Publishers*

"A Careful Man Dies" was first published in the November 1946 issue of *New Detective*; copyright © 1946 by Ray Bradbury.

"Sixty-Six" was first published in the December 2003 issue of *The Strand*; copyright © 2003 by Ray Bradbury.

FIRST EDITION

Designed by Stephanie Huntwork

Library of Congress Cataloging-in-Publication Data

Bradbury, Ray, 1920–
The cat's pajamas : stories / Ray Bradbury.—1st ed.
p. cm.
ISBN 0-06-058565-X
I. Title.
PS3503.R167C37 2004
813'.54—dc22 2004042617

05 06 07 08 JTC/RRD 10 9 8 7 6 5 4 3 2 1

For Maggie

Always and forever the cat's pajamas

REMEMBERING SKIP—

fine brother, good friend,
who shared those great early years in
Green Town, Illinois

*Thanks to Donn Albright for prowling
my basement and finding stories I'd
long since forgotten that I had written.
Still my golden retriever.*

CONTENTS

INTRODUCTION: ALIVE AND KICKING AND WRITING

WHAT IS THERE to say about my secret self, my subconscious, my creative demon, that writes these stories for me?

I will try to find some fresh insight into the process, which has kept me alive and kicking and writing for seventy years.

Two good examples of the way I've tried to work from the 1940s to now are my stories "Chrysalis" and "The Completist." (Note: The "Chrysalis" in this collection is different from the short story of the same name that was published in *Amazing Stories* magazine in 1946, and later collected in *S Is for Space*. I just liked the title so much that I used it twice.)

Back in the long summers of the 1940s, I, like my brother,

spent all my extra time at the beach. He was a real surfer, I was a body surfer, and in between times I lingered by the Santa Monica pier and got to know all the volleyball players and weight lifters. Among the friends I made were a few colored people (in those days, everyone did say "colored"; the terms "black" and "African-American" came years later).

I was intrigued by the thought that people of color might actually sunburn; it had never before crossed my mind. So the metaphor was there, "Chrysalis" was written, and now it is published for the first time. I wrote the story and put it away long years before the civil rights movement; it is a product of its era, and I believe that it stands the test of time.

"We'll Just Act Natural" is the result of my being raised in my grandmother's house, part time, by a black maid named Susan. She was a wonderful lady and I looked forward to her arrival once a week all during my childhood.

When my family went west in 1934, I lost contact with most of my Waukegan friends, including Susan. She wrote me a letter along the way asking if she could come out and be a maid for our family. Sadly, it was the middle of the Depression and my father was out of work and my brother joined the Civilian Conservation Corps in order not to be a burden to our family. We were dirt poor and hardly able to keep our own heads above water. I had to write to Susan and thank her for her kindness and wish her well in the future. This caused me to think about traveling back someday to visit my friends in Waukegan, and see Susan once again. It never happened, but the story is a result of my imagining the future and being not quite the human being I would like to be. I heard from Susan many years later; she had survived well during the later part of the Depression.

"The Completist" is another kind of story. Years ago, my wife, Maggie, and I encountered an incredible book collector and library founder on a voyage across the Atlantic. We spent hours with him and became intrigued with the stories he told of his fabulous life.

At the end of this encounter we were both shocked by something that occurred, and which you will find in the story.

I remembered that voyage and that gentleman for twenty years and did nothing with the metaphor that he offered.

During the last six weeks a strange and surprising thing has happened. My wife became ill in early November, wound up in the hospital, and passed away just before Thanksgiving. During her illness and in the time since, for the first time in seventy years my demon has lain quiet within me. My muse, my Maggie, was gone, and my demon did not know what to do.

As the days passed, and then the weeks, I began to wonder if I would ever write again; I was unaccustomed to waking in the morning and not having my private theater acting out its ideas inside my head.

But one morning a few days ago I woke and found "The Completist" gentleman sitting at the edge of my bed, waiting for me and saying, *At long last, write my story*.

Eagerly, for the first time in more than a month, I called my daughter Alexandra and dictated this story to her.

I hope you will make the comparison between "Chrysalis" and "The Completist" and find that though time has passed, my ability to know a metaphor when I see it has not changed.

My ability to write, of course, was much more primitive when I wrote "Chrysalis," but the idea itself is strong and worth considering.

"A Matter of Taste" is the result of encountering spiders during a good part of my life, either in the woodpile in Tucson or on the road to Mexico City, where we saw a spider so big we actually got out of the car to examine it. It was bigger than one of my hands and quite beautiful and furry. Back in California I realized all over again that every garage in Los Angeles contained several dozen black widow spiders, so you have to be careful that you don't get bitten by these poisonous creatures. Along the way you wonder what it's like to have a skeleton on the outside, instead of on the inside, so "A Matter of Taste" is an enlargement of that concept, where I portray a world of spiders on a far planet that are far brighter than the astronaut intruders who arrive to encounter them. This was the beginning of my considering a screenplay titled "It Came from Outer Space," which I wrote for Universal a few months later. So a story which involved my imagination resulted in my employment at a studio and the making of a rather nice film.

As for the other stories in this collection, most of them occurred almost instantly and I rushed to put them down.

I was signing books one day six months ago, with a young friend, and we began to talk about the Indian casinos that are situated around the United States. Quite suddenly I said to my young friend, "Wouldn't it be something if a bunch of drunken senators gambled away the United States to the head of an Indian casino?"

As soon as I said that, I cried, "Give me a pencil and paper," and wrote down the idea and finished the story a few hours later.

Glancing through a copy of *The New Yorker* six months ago I came across a series of photos of Okies, supposedly taken during the 1930s, when they were heading west on Route 66. Reading further, I discovered they were not Okies at all, but New York models dressed up in ancient clothing and posed in New York City, sometime during the past year. I was so astounded and angered by this revelation—how could that tragic chapter of our history become fodder for a fashion shoot!?—that I wrote the story "Sixty-Six."

This book is also full of my love of my favorite writers. I have never in my life been jealous or envious of my great loves like F. Scott Fitzgerald, Melville, Poe, Wilde, and the rest. I've only wanted to join them on the shelves of libraries.

It follows that I'd been so worried about the mind and creativity of Fitzgerald that time and again I have invented time machines to go back and save him from himself; an impossible task, of course, but my love demanded it.

In this collection you will find me as a defender of a faith, helping Scotty to finish work he should have finished and telling him again and again not to worship money and to stay away from the motion picture studios.

Traveling on the freeway to Pasadena several years ago I saw the fabulous graffiti on the cement walls and on the overhead bridges, where anonymous artists had hung upside down to create their miraculous murals. The idea so intrigued me that at the end of the journey I wrote "*Olé,* Orozco! Siqueiros, *Sí*!"

The story about Lincoln's funeral train, "The John Wilkes Booth/Warner Brothers/MGM/NBC Funeral Train," would seem quite obvious, since we live in an age when publicity seems to be a way of life, the realities of history are ignored, and villains, rather than heroes, are celebrated.

"All My Enemies Are Dead" is a fairly obvious story. As we get older we discover that not only do our friends vanish in time, but the enemies who bullied us—in grade school, in high school—fall away, and we find that we have no hostile remembrances to remember! I've carried that concept to the very end.

"The R.B., G.K.C., and G.B.S. Forever Orient Express" is not a story, per se, but more a story-poem, and it is a perfect demonstration of my complete love for the library and its authors from the time I was eight years old. I didn't make it to college, so the library became my meeting place with people like G. K. Chesterton and Shaw and the rest of that fabulous group who inhabited the stacks. My dream was to one day walk into the library and see one of my books leaning against one of theirs. I never was jealous of my heroes, nor did I envy them, I only wanted to trot along as lapdog to their fame. The poem came out one day all in one continuous roll so that I as a quiet mouse could ride along half-seen and listen to their fabulous talk. If anything represents my goal in life over a period, it is this poem, which is why I chose to include it here.

In sum, most of these stories have seized me at various times and would not let me go until I nailed them down.

My demon speaks. I hope that you will listen.

THE CAT'S PAJAMAS

CHRYSALIS

1946–1947

LONG AFTER MIDNIGHT he arose and looked at the bottles fresh from their cartons, and put his hands up to touch them and strike a match gently to read the white labels, while his folks slept unaware in the next room. Below the hill on which their house stood the sea rolled in and while whispering the magic names of the lotions to himself he could hear the tides washing the rocks and the sand. The names lay easy on his tongue: *MEMPHIS WHITE OIL*, *Guaranteed*, *Tennessee Lotion Salve* . . . *HIGGEN'S BLEACH BONE WHITE SOAP*—the names that were like sunlight burning away dark, like water bleaching linens. He would uncork them and sniff them and pour a little on his hands and rub them together and hold his hand in match light to see how soon he would have hands like white cotton gloves. When nothing happened, he consoled himself that perhaps tomorrow night, or the next, and back in bed he would lie with his eyes upon the bottles, racked like giant green glass beetles above him, glinting in the faint streetlight.

Why am I doing this? he thought. Why?

"Walter?" That was his mother calling softly, far away.

"Yes'm?"

"You awake, Walter?"

"Yes'm."

"You better go to sleep," she said.

IN THE MORNING he went down for his first view, close up, of the constant sea. It was a wonder to him, for he had never seen one. They came from a little town deep in Alabama, all dust and heat, with dry creeks and mud holes, but no river, no lake nearby, nothing much at all unless you traveled, and this was the first traveling they had done, coming to California in a dented Ford, singing quietly along the way. Just before starting the trip Walter had finished out a year's time saving his money and sent off for the twelve bottles of magical lotion that had arrived only the day before they left. So he had had to pack them into cartons and carry them across the meadows and deserts of the states, secretly trying one or the other of them in shanties and restrooms along the way. He had sat up front in the car, his head back, his eyes closed, taking the sun, lotion on his face, waiting to be bleached as white as milkstone. "I can see it," he said, each night, to himself. "Just a little bit."

"Walter," said his mother. "What's that smell? What you wearing?"

"Nothing, Mom, nothing."

Nothing? He walked in the sand and stopped by the green waters and pulled one of the flasks from his pocket and let a thin twine of whitish fluid coil upon his palm before he smoothed it over his face and arms. He would lie like a raven by the sea all day today and let the sun burn away his darkness. Maybe he would plow into the waves and let them churn him, as a washing machine churns a dark rag, and let it spit him out on the sand, gasping to dry and bake in the sun until he lay there like the thin skeleton of some old beast, chalk-white and fresh and clean.

GUARANTEED said the red letters on the bottle. The word flamed in his mind. *GUARANTEED!*

"Walter," his mother would say, shocked. "What happened to you? Is that *you,* son? Why, you're like milk, son, you're like snow!"

It was hot. Walter eased himself down against the boardwalk and took off his shoes. Behind him, a hot dog stand sent up shimmers of fried air, the smell of onions and hot rolls and frankfurters. A man with a grained, ropy face looked out at Walter, and Walter nodded shyly, looking away. A moment later a wicket gate slammed and Walter heard the blunt footsteps approaching. The man stood looking down at Walter, a silver spatula in one hand, a cook's cap on his head, greasy and gray.

"You better get along," he said.

"I beg your pardon, sir?"

"I said the niggers' beach is down there." The man tilted his head in that direction without looking that way, looking only at Walter. "I don't want you standing around in front of my place."

Walter blinked up at the man, surprised. "But this is California," he said.

"You tryin' to get tough with me?" asked the man.

"No, sir, I just said this ain't the South, sir."

"Anywhere where I am is South," said the man and walked back into his hot dog stand to slap some burgers on the griddle and stamp them flat with his spatula, glaring out at Walter.

Walter turned his long easy body around and walked north. The wonder and curiosity of this beach-place returned to him in a tide of water and sifting sand. At the very end of the boardwalk he stopped and squinted down.

A white boy lay lazily curled into a quiet posture on the white sands.

A puzzled light shone in Walter's large eyes. All whites were strange, but this one was all the strangeness of them all rolled into one. Walter lapped one brown foot over the other, watching. The white boy seemed to be waiting for something down there on the sand.

The white boy kept scowling at his own arms, stroking them, peering over his shoulder, staring down the incline of his back, peering at his belly and his firm clean legs.

Walter let himself down off the boardwalk, uneasily. Very carefully he pedaled the sand and stood nervously, hopefully over the white boy, licking his lips, throwing a shadow down.

The white boy sprawled like a stringless puppet, relaxed. The long shadow crossed his hands, and he glanced up at Walter, leisurely, then looked away, then back again.

Walter walked closer, smiled, self-consciously, and stared around as if it was someone else the white boy was looking at.

The boy grinned. "Hi."

Walter said, very quietly, "Hello there."

"Swell day."

"It most certainly is," said Walter, smiling.

He did not move. He stood with his long delicate fingers at his sides, and he let the wind run down the dark economical rows of hair on his head, and finally the white boy said, "Flop down!"

"Thanks," said Walter, immediately obeying.

The boy moved his eyes in all directions. "Not many guys down today."

"End of the season," said Walter, carefully.

"Yeah. School started a week ago."

A pause. Walter said, "You graduate?"

"Last June. Been working all summer; didn't have time to get down to the beach."

"Making up for lost time?"

"Yeah. Don't know if I can pick up much tan in two weeks, though. Got to go to Chicago October first."

"Oh," said Walter, nodding. "I saw you here, I did, every day now. I wondered about that."

The boy sighed, lazing his head on crossed arms. "Nothing like the beach. What's your name? Mine's Bill."

"I'm Walter. Hello, Bill."

"Hi, Walt."

A wave came in on the shore, softly, shining.

"You like the beach?" asked Walter.

"Sure, you shoulda seen me summer before last!"

"I bet you got all burnt up," said Walter.

"Heck, I *never* burn. I just get blacker and blacker. I get black as a nig—" The white boy faltered, stopped. Color rose in his face, flushed. "I get plenty dark," he ended lamely, not looking at Walter, embarrassed.

To show he didn't mind, Walter laughed softly, almost sadly, shaking his head.

Bill looked at him, queerly. "What's funny?"

"Nothing," said Walter, looking at the white boy's long pale arms and half-pale legs and stomach. "Nothing whatsoever."

Bill stretched out like a white cat to take in the sun, to let it strike through to every relaxed bone. "Take off your shirt, Walt. Get yourself some sun."

"No, I can't do that," said Walter.

"Why not?"

"I'd get sunburned," said Walter.

"Ho!" cried the white boy. Then he rolled swiftly over to hush himself with one hand cupping his mouth. He lowered his eyes, raised them again. "Sorry. I thought you were joking."

Walter bent his head, blinking his long beautiful lashes.

"That's all right," he said. "I know you thought that."

Bill seemed to see Walt for the first time. Acutely self-conscious, Walter tucked his bare feet under his hams, because it had suddenly struck him how much like tan rain-rubbers they looked. Tan rain-rubbers worn against some storm that never seemed to quite come.

Bill was confused. "I never thought of that. I didn't know."

"Why, we sure do. All I got to do," said Walter, "is peel off my shirt and *boom* I'm all blisters! *Sure,* we sunburn."

"I'll be darned." Bill said, "I'll be gosh-darned. I should *know* these things. I guess we never think much about things like that."

Walter sifted sand in the palm of one hand. "No," he said, slowly, "I don't guess you do." He rose. "Well, I better get on up to the hotel. Got to help my mom in the kitchen."

"See you again, Walt."

"Sure thing. Tomorrow and the next day."

"Okay. So long."

Walter waved and walked swiftly up the hill. At the top he squinted back. Bill still lay on the sand, waiting for something.

Walter bit his lips, shook his fingers at the ground.

"Man," he said aloud, "that boy is *crazy*!"

WHEN WALTER WAS a very little boy he'd tried to reverse things. Teacher at school had pointed to a picture of a fish, and said:

"Notice how colorless and bleached this fish is from swimming deep in Mammoth Cave for generations. It is blind and needs no seeing organs, and—"

That same afternoon, years ago, Walter had rushed home from school and eagerly hid himself upstairs in Mr. Hampden's, the caretaker's, attic. Outside, the hot Alabama sun beat down. In the mothball darkness, Walter crouched, heard his heart drum. A mouse rustled across the dirty plankings.

He had it all figured out. White man working in the sun turned black. Black boy hiding in the dark, turn white. Why, *sure*! It was reasonable, wasn't it? If one thing happened one way, then the other thing would happen its own way, wouldn't it?

He stayed in that attic until hunger brought him down the stairs.

It was night. The stars shone.

He stared at his hands.

They were still brown.

But just wait until morning! This didn't count! You couldn't see the change at night, no, sir! Just wait, just wait! Sucking in his breath, he ran the rest of the way down the steps of the old house and hurried to his mama's shack down in the grove and sneaked into bed, keeping his hands in his pockets, keeping his eyes shut. Thinking hard as he went to sleep.

In the morning he awoke and a cage of light from the one small widow enclosed him.

His very dark arms and hands lay upon the tattered quilt, unchanged.

He let out a great sigh, and buried his face in his pillow.

WALTER WAS DRAWN back to the boardwalk each afternoon, always careful to give the hot dog proprietor and his grill a wide go-around.

A great thing was happening, thought Walter. A great change, a progression. He would watch the details of this dying summer, and it would give him much to think of. He would try to understand the summer all the way to the end of it. Autumn rose in a tidal wave, poised over him, ready to drop, suspended.

Bill and Walter talked each day, and afternoons passed, and their two arms lying near each other began to resemble one another in an oddly pleasing way to Walter, who watched, fascinated with this thing occurring, this thing Bill had planned and so patiently bided his time for.

Bill traced sand patterns with one pale hand that day by day became a darker hand. Each finger was dyed by the sun.

On Saturday and Sunday, more white boys appeared. Walter walked away, but Bill yelled for him to stay, what the heck, what the heck! And Walter joined them playing volleyball.

Summer had plunged them all into sand-flame and green water-flame until they were rinsed and lacquered with darkness. For the first time in his life, Walter felt a part of people. They'd chosen to cloak themselves in his skin and they danced, growing dark, on each side of the high net, tossing the ball and their laughter back and forth, wrestling with Walter, joking with him, tossing him into the sea.

Finally, one day Bill slapped his hand to Walter's wrist bone and cried, "Look here, Walter!"

Walter looked.

"I'm darker than you are, Walt!" cried Bill, amazed.

"I'll be darned, I'll be gosh-darned," murmured Walter, moving his eyes from wrist to wrist. "Umnh-umnh. Yes, sir, you *are*, Bill. You *sure* are."

Bill left his fingers on Walter's wrist, a sudden stunned expression on his face, half scowling, lower lip loosened, and thoughts starting to shift places in his eyes. He jerked his hand away with a sharp laugh and looked out to sea.

"Tonight I'm wearing my white sport shirt. It sure looks snazzy. The white shirt and my tan—boy-oh-boy!"

"I bet that looks nice," said Walter, looking to see what Bill was gazing at. "Lots of colored folks wear *black* clothes and wine-colored shirts to make their faces seem whiter."

"Is that so, Walt? I didn't know that."

Bill seemed uneasy, as if he'd thought of something he couldn't handle. As if it was a brilliant idea he said to Walter, "Hey, here's some dough. Go buy us a coupla dogs."

Walter smiled appreciatively. "That hot dog man don't like me."

"Take the dough and go, anyhow. To hell with him."

"All right," said Walter, with reluctance. "You want everything on yours?"

"The works!"

Walter loped across the hot sands. Leaping up to the walk he passed into the odorous shadow of the stand where he stood tall and dignified and flute-lipped. "Two hot dogs, with everything on them, to go out, please," he said.

The man behind the counter had his spatula in his hand. He just examined Walter inch by inch, in great detail, with that spatula twitching in his lean fingers. He didn't speak.

When Walter got tired of standing there, he turned and walked out.

Jingling the money on his big palm, Walter walked along, pretending he didn't care. The jingle stopped when Bill caught hold of him.

"What happened, Walt?"

"That man just looked at me and looked at me, that's all."

Bill turned him around. "Come on! We'll get those hot dogs or I'll know why in hell not!"

Walter held off. "I don't want no trouble."

"Okay. Damn it. I'll get the dogs. You wait here."

Bill ran over and leaned against the shadowy counter.

Walter saw and heard plainly all that happened in the next ten seconds.

The hot dog man snapped his head up to glare at Bill. He shouted, "Damn you, blackie. You here again!"

There was a silence.

Bill leaned across the counter, waiting.

The hot dog man laughed hastily. "Well, I'll be damned. Hello, *Bill*! There's a glare from the water—you looked just like— What'll you have?"

Bill seized the man's elbow. "I don't get it? I'm darker than him. Why are you kissing *my* butt?"

The proprietor labored at his answer. "Hey, Bill, you standing there in the glare—"

"God damn you to hell!"

Bill came out into the bright light, pale under his suntan, took Walter's elbow and started walking.

"Come on, Walt. I'm not hungry."

"That's funny," said Walt. "Neither am I."

THE TWO WEEKS ended. Autumn came. There was a cold salt fog for two days, and Walter thought he'd never see Bill again. He walked down along the boardwalk, alone. It was very quiet. No horns honking. The wooden frontings of the final and last hot dog stand had been slammed down and nailed fast, and a great lonely wind ran along the chilling gray beach.

On Tuesday there was a brief bit of sunlight and, sure enough, there was Bill, stretched out, all alone on the empty beach.

"Thought I'd come down just one last time," he said as Walt sat down beside him. "Well, I won't see you again."

"Going to Chicago?"

"Yeah. No more sun here, anyway; at least not the kind of sun I like. Better get along east."

"I suppose you better," said Walter.

"It was a good two weeks," said Bill.

Walter nodded. "It was a very *fine* two weeks."

"I sure got tan."

"You sure did."

"It's starting to come off now, though," said Bill, regretfully. "Wish I'd had time to make it a good permanent one." He peered over his shoulder at his back and made some gestures at it with elbows bent, fingers clutching. "Look, Walt, this damn stuff is peeling off, and it itches. You mind taking off some of the stuff?"

"I don't mind," said Walter. "Turn around."

Bill turned silently, and Walter, reaching out, eyes shining, gently pulled off a strip of skin.

Piece by piece, flake after flake, strip by strip, he peeled the dark skin off of Bill's muscled back, shoulder blades, neck, spine, bringing out the pink naked white underneath.

When he finished, Bill looked nude and lonely and small and Walter realized that he had done something to Bill, but that Bill was accepting it philosophically, not worried about it, and a great light shone in Walter instantly, out of the whole summer's time!

He had done something to Bill that was right and natural and there was no way of escaping or getting around it, that was the way it was and had to be. Bill had waited the summer through and thought he had something, but it wasn't really there all the time. He just thought it was there.

The wind blew away the flakes of skin.

"You been lying here all July and August for that," said Walter, slowly. He dropped a fragment. "And there it goes. I been waiting all my life and it goes to the same place." He turned his back proudly to Bill and then, half sad, half happy, but at peace he said:

"Now, let's see you peel some offa me!"

THE ISLAND

1952

THE WINTER NIGHT DRIFTED by lamplit windows in white bits and pieces. Now the procession marched evenly, now fluttered and spun. But there was a continual sifting and settling, which never stopped filling a deep abyss with silence.

The house was locked and bolted at every seam, window, door, and hatch. Lamps bloomed softly in each room. The house held its breath, drowsed and warm. Radiators sighed. A refrigerator hummed quietly. In the library, under the lime green hurricane lamp, a white hand moved, a pen scratched, a face bent to the ink, which dried in the false summer air.

Upstairs in bed, an old woman lay reading. Across the upper hall, her daughter sorted linen in a cupboard room. On the attic floor above, a son, half through thirty years, tapped delicately at a typewriter, added yet another paper ball to the growing heap on the rug.

Downstairs, the kitchen maid finished the supper wine-glasses, placed them with clear bell sounds onto shelves, wiped her hands, arranged her hair, and reached for the light switch.

It was then that all five inhabitants of the snowing winter night house heard the unusual sound.

The sound of a window breaking.

It was like the cracking of moon-colored ice on a midnight pond.

The old woman sat up in bed. Her youngest daughter stopped sorting linens. About to crumple a typewritten page, the son froze, the paper shut in his fist.

In the library, the second daughter caught her breath, let the dark ink dry with almost an audible hiss, halfway down the page.

The kitchen maid stood, fingers on the light switch.

Not a sound.

Silence.

And the whisper of the cold wind from some far broken window, wandering the halls.

Each head turned in its separate room, looked first at the faintest stir of carpet nap where the wind stroked in under each breathing door. Then they snapped their gazes to the brass door locks.

Each door had its own bulwarking, each its arrangements

of snap-bolts, chain-locks, bars, and keys. The mother, in those years when her eccentricities had spun them like tops until their sense flew away, had supervised the doors as if each were a precious and wonderful new still life.

In the years before illness had stuffed her unceremoniously in bed, she had professed fears of any room that could not *instantly* become a fortress! A houseful of women (son Robert rarely descended from his crow's nest) needed swift defenses against the blind greeds, envies, and rapes of a world only a bit less feverish with lust in winter.

So ran her theory.

"We'll never need *that* many locks!" Alice had protested years ago.

"There'll come a day," the mother replied, "you'll thank God for one single solid Yale lock."

"But all a robber has to do," said Alice, "is smash a window, undo the sill locks and—"

"Break a window! And *warn* us? Nonsense!"

"It would all be so simple if we only kept our money in the *bank*."

"Again, nonsense! I learned in 1929 to keep hard cash from soft hands! There's a gun under my pillow and our money under my bed! *I'm* the First National Bank of Oak Green Island!"

"A bank worth forty thousand dollars?!"

"Hush! Why don't you stand at the landing and tell all the fishermen? Besides, it's not just cash that the fiends would come for. Yourself, Madeline—*me*!"

"Mother, Mother. Old maids, let's face it."

"Women, never forget, *women*. Where are the *other* pistols?"

"One in each room, Mother."

And so the home-grown artillery was primed and set, the hatches dogged and undogged from season to season, year to year. An intercommunication phone circuit, using batteries, was wired upstairs and down. The daughters had accepted the phones, smiling, it at least saved shouting up the stairwells.

"Simultaneously," said Alice, "why not cut off our outside phone? It's long past time anyone called from the town across the lake to either Madeline or me."

"Pull out the phone!" said Madeline. "It costs like hell each month! Who could *we* possibly want to call over there?"

"Boors," said Robert, heading for the attic. "All of them."

And now, on this deep winter night, the one single and solitary sound. The shattering of a windowpane, like a wineglass thinly burst, like the breaking of a long warm winter dream.

All five inhabitants of this island house became white statues.

Peeking in windows at each room, one would have imagined museum galleries. Each animal, stuffed with terror, displayed in a last instant of awareness; recognition. There was a light in each glass eye, like that found and forever remembered from a noon glade when a deer, startled and motionless, slowly turned its head to gaze down the long cold barrel of a steel rifle.

Each of the five found their attention fixed to the doors.

Each saw that an entire continent separated their bed or chair from those doors waiting, ready to be locked. An inconsequential yardage to the body. But a psychological immensity to the mind. While they were flinging themselves the short distance, the long distance to slide the bolts, turn the keys, might not some *thing* in the hall leap a similar space to crack the still-unlocked door!?

This thought, with hair-trigger swiftness, flashed through each head. It held them. It would not set them free.

A second, comforting thought came next.

It's nothing, it said. The wind broke the window. A tree branch fell, yes! Or a snowball, thrown by some winter-haunted child, soundless in the night, on his way nowhere. . . .

ALL FIVE MEMBERS of the house arose in unison.

The halls shook with the wind. A whiteness flaked in the family's faces and snowed in their stricken eyes. All made ready to seize their private doors, open, peer out and cry, "It *was* a falling tree limb, yes!" when they heard yet another sound.

A metal rattling.

And then, a window, somewhere, like the cruel edge of a giant guillotine, began to rise.

It slid in its raw grooves. It gaped a great mouth to let winter in.

Every house door knocked and yammered its hinges and sills.

The gust snuffed out lamps in every room.

"No electricity!" said Mother, years ago. "No gifts from the town! Self-sufficiency's our ticket! Give and take nothing."

Her voice faded in the past.

No sooner had the oil lamps whiffed out than fear took fire to blaze brighter than logs and hearths, than slumbering coals, in each room.

Alice felt it burn from her cheeks with a ghastly light. She could have read books by the terror that flamed in her brow.

There seemed only one thing to do.

Rushing en masse, each room, a duplicate of the one above or below, four people flung themselves to their doors, to scrabble locks, throw bolts, attach chains, twist keys!

"Safe!" they cried. "Locked and safe!"

All save one moved this way: the maid. She lived but a few hours each day in this outrageous home, untouched by the mother's wild panics and fears. Made practical with years of living in the town beyond the wide moat of lawn, hedge, and wall, she debated only an instant. Then she performed what should have been a saving, but became a despairing, gesture.

Yanking wide the kitchen door she rushed into the main lower hallway. From far off in darkness the wind blew from a cold dragon's mouth.

The others will be out! she thought.

Quickly, she called their names.

"Miss Madeline, Miss Alice, Mrs. Benton, Mr. Robert!"

Then turning, she plunged down the hall toward the blowing darkness of the open window.

"Miss Madeline!"

Madeline, pinned like Jesus to her linen-room door, rescrabbled the locks.

"Miss Alice!"

In the library, where her pale letters capered in darkness, like drunken moths, Alice fell back from her own shut door, found matches, relit the double hurricanes. Her head beat like a heart gorged, pressing her eyes out, gasping her lips, sealing her ears so nothing was heard but a wild pulse and the hollow in-suck of her breath.

"Mrs. Benton!"

The old one squirmed in bed, worked her hands over her face, to reshape the melted flesh into a shocked expression it most needed. Then her fingers splayed out at the unlocked door. "Fool! Damn fool! Someone lock my door! Alice, Robert, Madeline!"

"Alice, Robert, Madeline!" the echoes blew in the unlit halls.

"Mr. Robert!"

The maid's voice summoned him from the floor, trembling.

Then, one by one, they heard the maid cry out. One small dismayed and accusing cry.

After that the snow touched the roof of the house softly.

They all stood, knowing what that silence meant. They waited for some new sound.

Someone, treading slowly on nightmare softness, as if barefoot, drifted along the halls. They felt the house shift with the weight now here, now there, now farther along.

Two phones stood on a far library desk. Alice seized one, chattered the hook, cried, "Operator! Police!"

But then she remembered: *No one will call Madeline and me now. Tell the Bell Company to pull the phone. There's no one in town we know.*

Be practical, Mother had said. *Leave the phone itself here, in case we ever decide to reconnect.*

"Operator!"

She threw the instrument down and blinked at it as if it were some stubborn beast she had asked to do the simplest trick. She glanced at the window. Push it up, lean out, *scream*! Ah, but the neighbors were locked in, warm and apart and separate and lost, and the wind screaming, too, and winter all around, and night. It would be like shouting to graveyards.

"Robert, Alice, Madeline, Robert, Alice, Madeline!"

The mother, screaming, blind idiocy.

"Lock my door! Robert, Alice, Madeline!"

I hear, thought Alice. We all hear. And *he'll* hear her too.

She grabbed the second phone, gave its button three sharp jabs.

"Madeline, Alice, Robert!" Her voice blew through the halls.

"Mother!" cried Alice over the phone. "Don't scream,

don't tell him where you *are,* don't tell him what he doesn't even know!" Alice jabbed the button again.

"Robert, Alice, Madeline!"

"Pick up the phone, Mother, please, pick—"

Click.

"Hello, Operator." Her mother's raw shrieking voice. "Save me! The locks!"

"Mother, this is Alice! Quiet, he'll hear you!"

"Oh, God! Alice, oh God, the door! I can't get out of bed! Silly, awful, all the locks and no way to get *to* them!"

"Put out your lamp!"

"Help me, Alice!"

"I am helping. Listen! Find your gun. Blow out your light. Hide under your bed! *Do* that!"

"Oh, God! Alice, come lock my door!"

"Mother, listen!"

"Alice, Alice!" Madeline's voice. "What's happened? I'm afraid!"

Another voice. "Alice!"

"Robert!"

They shrieked and yelled.

"No," said Alice. "Quiet, one at a time! Before it's too late. *All* of us. Do you *hear*? Get your guns, open your doors, come out in the hall. It's us, *all* of us, against him. Yes?!"

Robert sobbed.

Madeline wailed.

"Alice, Madeline, children, save your mother!"

"Mother, shut up!" Alice swayed and chanted. "Open your doors. *All* of us. We can *do* it! Now!"

"He'll get me!" screamed Madeline.

"No, no," said Robert. "It's no use, no use!"

"The door, my door, unlocked," cried the mother.

"Listen, all of you!"

"My door!" said the mother. "Oh God! It's opening, *now*!"

There was a scream in the halls and the same scream on the phone.

The others stared at the phones in their hands where only their hearts beat.

"Mother!"

A door slammed upstairs.

The scream stopped suddenly.

"Mother!"

If only she hadn't yelled, thought Alice. If only she hadn't showed him the way.

"Madeline, Robert! Your guns. I'll count five and we'll *all* rush out! One, two, three—"

Robert groaned.

"Robert!"

He fell to the floor, the phone in his fist. His door was still locked. His heart stopped. The phone in his fist shouted, "Robert!" He lay still.

"He's at my door now!" said Madeline, high in the winter house.

"Fire through the door! Shoot!"

"He won't get *me,* he won't have his way with *me*!"

"Madeline, listen! Shoot through the door!"

"He's fumbling with the lock, he'll get in!"

"Madeline!"

One shot.

One shot and only one.

Alice stood in the library alone, staring at the cold phone in her hand. It was now completely silent.

Suddenly she saw that stranger in the dark, upstairs, outside a door, in the hall, scratching softly, smiling at the panel.

The shot!

The stranger in the dark peering down. And from under the locked door, slowly, a small stream of blood. Blood flowing quietly, very bright, in a tiny stream. All this, Alice saw. All this she knew, hearing a dark movement in the upstairs hall as someone moved from room to room, trying doors and finding silence.

"Madeline," she said to the phone, numbly. "Robert!" She called their names, uselessly. "Mother!" She shut her eyes. "Why didn't you *listen*? If we had *all* of us at the very *first*—run out—"

Silence.

Snow fell in silent whirls and cornucopias, heaped itself in lavish quietness upon the lawn. She was now alone.

Stumbling to the window, she unlocked it, forced it up, unhooked the storm window beyond, pushed it out. Then she straddled, half in the silent warm world of the house, half out into the snowing night. She sat a long moment, gazing at the locked library door. The brass knob twisted once.

Fascinated, she watched it turn. Like a bright eye it fixed her.

She almost wanted to walk over, undo the latch, and with a bow, beckon in the night, the shape of terror, so as to know the face of such a one who, with hardly a knock, had razed an island fort. She found the gun in her hand, raised it, pointed it at the door, shivering.

The brass knob turned clockwise, counterclockwise. Darkness stood in darkness beyond, blowing. Clockwise, counterclockwise. With an unseen smile above.

Eyes shut she fired three times!

When she opened her eyes she saw that her shots had gone wide. One into the wall, another at the bottom of the door, a third at the top. She stared a moment at her coward's hand, and flung the gun away.

The doorknob turned this way, that. It was the last thing she saw. The bright doorknob shining like an eye.

Leaning out, she fell into the snow.

RETURNING WITH THE POLICE hours later, she saw her footsteps in the snow, running away from silence.

She and the sheriff and his men stood under the empty trees, gazing at the house.

It seemed warm and comfortable, once again brightly

lighted, a world of radiance and cheer in a bleak landscape. The front door stood wide to the blowing snows.

"Jesus," said the sheriff. "He must have just opened up the front door and strolled *out,* damn, not caring *who* saw! Christ, what *nerve*!"

Alice moved. A thousand white moths flicked her eyes. She blinked and her eyes fixed in a stare. Then slowly, softly, her throat fluttered.

She began a laugh that ended with a muffled sobbing.

"Look!" she cried. "Oh, *look*!"

They looked, and then saw the second path of footprints which came neatly down the front porch stairs into the white soft velvet snow. Evenly spaced, with a certain serenity, these footprints could be seen where they marched off across the front yard, confident and deep, vanishing away into the cold night and snowing town.

"*His* footsteps." Alice bent and put out her hand. She measured then tried to cover them with a thrust of her numb fingers. She cried out.

"*His* footsteps. Oh God, what a little man! Do you see the size of them, do you *see*! My God, what a *little* man!"

And even as she crouched there, on hands and knees, sobbing, the wind and the winter and the night did her a gentle kindness. Even as she watched, the snow fell into and around and over the footprints, smoothing and filling and erasing them until at last, with no trace, with no memory of their smallness, they were gone.

Then, and only then, did she stop crying.

Sometime Before Dawn

1950

It was the crying late at night, perhaps, the hysteria, and then the sobbing violently, and after it had passed away into a sighing, I could hear the husband's voice through the wall. "There, there," he would say, "there, there."

I would lie upon my back in my night bed and listen and wonder, and the calendar on my wall said August 2002. And the man and his wife, young, both about thirty, and fresh-looking, with light hair and blue eyes, but lines around their mouths, had just moved into the rooming house where I took my meals and worked as a janitor in the downtown library.

Every night and every night it would be the same thing, the wife crying, and the husband quieting her with his soft voice beyond my wall. I would strain to hear what started it, but I could never tell. It wasn't anything he said, I was positive of this, or anything he did. I was almost certain, in fact, that it started all by itself, late at night, about two o'clock. She would wake up, I theorized, and I would hear that first terrorized shriek and then the long crying. It made me sad. As old as I am, I hate to hear a woman cry.

I remember the first night they came here, a month ago, an August evening here in this town deep in Illinois, all the houses dark and everyone on the porches licking ice-cream bars. I remember walking through the kitchen downstairs and standing in the old smells of cooking and hearing but not seeing the dog lapping water from the pan under the stove, a nocturnal sound, like water in a cave. And I walked on through to the parlor and in the dark, with his face devilish pink from exertion, Mr. Fiske, the landlord, was fretting over the air conditioner, which, damned thing, refused to work. Finally in the hot night he wandered outside onto the mosquito porch—it was made for mosquitoes only, Mr. Fiske averred, but went there anyway.

I went out onto the porch and sat down and unwrapped a cigar to fire away my own special mosquitoes, and there were Grandma Fiske and Alice Fiske and Henry Fiske and Joseph Fiske and Bill Fiske and six other boarders and roomers, all unwrapping Eskimo pies.

It was then that the man and his wife, as suddenly as if they had sprung up out of the wet dark grass, appeared at the bottom of the steps, looking up at us like the spectators in a summer night circus. They had no luggage. I always remembered that. They had no luggage. And their clothes did not seem to fit them.

"Is there a place for food and sleep?" said the man, in a halting voice.

Everyone was startled. Perhaps I was the one who saw them first, then Mrs. Fiske smiled and got out of her wicker chair and came forward. "Yes, we have rooms."

"How much is the money?" asked the man in the broiling dark.

"Twenty dollars a day, with meals."

They did not seem to understand. They looked at each other.

"Twenty dollars," said Grandma.

"We'll move into here," said the man.

"Don't you want to look first?" asked Mrs. Fiske.

They came up the steps, looking back, as if someone was following them.

That was the first night of the crying.

Breakfast was served every morning at seven-thirty, large, toppling stacks of pancakes, huge jugs of syrup, islands of butter, toast, many pots of coffee, and cereal if you wished. I was working on my cereal when the new couple came down the stairs, slowly. They did not come into the dining room immediately, but I had a sense they were just looking at everything. Since Mrs. Fiske was busy I went in to fetch them, and there they were, the man and wife, just looking out the front window, looking and looking at the green grass and the big elm trees and the blue sky. Almost as if they had never seen them before.

"Good morning," I said.

They ran their fingers over antimacassars or through the bead-curtain-rain that hung in the dining room doorway. Once I thought I saw them both smile very broadly at some secret thing. I asked them their name. At first they puzzled over this but then said,

"Smith."

I introduced them around to everyone eating and they sat and looked at the food and at last began to eat.

They spoke very little, and only when spoken to, and I had an opportunity to remark the beauty in their faces, for they had fine and graceful bone structures in their chins and cheeks and brows, good straight noses, and clear eyes, but always that tiredness about the mouths.

Half through the breakfast, an event occurred to which I must call special attention. Mr. Britz, the garage mechanic, said, "Well, the president has been out fund-raising again today, I see by the paper."

The stranger, Mr. Smith, snorted angrily. "That terrible man! I've always hated Westercott."

Everyone looked at him. I stopped eating.

Mrs. Smith frowned at her husband. He coughed slightly and went on eating.

Mr. Britz scowled momentarily, and then we all finished breakfast, but I remember it now. What Mr. Smith had said was, "That terrible man! I've always hated Westercott."

I never forgot.

THAT NIGHT SHE CRIED AGAIN, as if she was lost in the woods, and I stayed awake for an hour, thinking.

There were so many things I suddenly wanted to ask them. And yet it was almost impossible to see them, for they stayed locked in the room constantly.

The next day, however, was Saturday. I caught them momentarily in the garden looking at the pink roses, just standing and looking, not touching, and I said, "A fine day!"

"A wonderful, wonderful day!" they both cried, almost in unison, and then laughed embarrassedly.

"Oh, it can't be *that* good." I smiled.

"You don't know how good it is, you don't know how wonderful it is—you can't possibly guess," she said, and then quite suddenly there were tears in her eyes.

I stood bewildered. "I'm sorry," I said. "Are you all right?"

"Yes, yes." She blew her nose and went off a distance to pick a few flowers. I stood looking at the apple tree hung with red fruit, and at last I got the courage to inquire, "May I ask where you're from, Mr. Smith?"

"The United States," he said slowly, as if piecing the words together.

"Oh, I was rather under the impression that—"

"We were from another country?"

"Yes."

"We are from the United States."

"What's your business, Mr. Smith?"

"I *think*."

"I see," I said, for all the answers were less than satisfactory. "Oh, by the way, what's Westercott's first name?"

"Lionel," said Mr. Smith, and then stared at me. The color left his face. He turned in a panic. "Please," he cried, softly. "Why do you ask these questions?" They hurried into the house before I could apologize. From the stair window they looked out at me as if I were the spy of the world. I felt contemptible and ashamed.

ON SUNDAY MORNING I helped clean the house. Tapping on the Smiths' door I received no answer. Listening, for the first time, I heard the tickings, the little clicks and murmurs of numerous clocks working away quietly in the room. I stood entranced. Tick-tick-tick-tick-tick! Two, no, *three* clocks. When I opened their door to fetch their wastepaper basket, I saw the clocks, arrayed, on the bureau, on the windowsill, and by the nightstand, small and large clocks, all set to this hour of the late morning, ticking like a roomful of insects.

So *many* clocks. But why? I wondered. Mr. Smith had *said* he was a *thinker*.

I took the wastebasket down to the incinerator. Inside the basket, as I was dumping it, I found one of her handkerchiefs. I fondled it for a moment, smelling the flower fragrance. Then I tossed it onto the fire.

It did not burn.

I poked at it and pushed it far back in the fire.

But the handkerchief would not burn.

In my room I took out my cigar lighter and touched it to the handkerchief. It would not burn, nor could I tear it.

And then I considered their clothing. I realized why it had seemed peculiar. The cut was regular for men and women in this season, but in their coats and shirts and dresses and shoes, there was not one blessed seam anywhere!

They came back out later that afternoon to walk in the garden. Peering from my high window I saw them standing together, holding hands, talking earnestly.

It was then that the terrifying thing happened.

A roar filled the sky. The woman looked into the sky, screamed, put her hands to her face, and collapsed. The man's face turned white, he stared blindly at the sun, and he fell to his knees calling to his wife to get up, get up, but she lay there, hysterically.

By the time I got downstairs to help, they had vanished. They had evidently run around one side of the house while I had gone around the other. The sky was empty, the roar had dwindled.

Why, I thought, should a simple, ordinary sound of a plane flying unseen in the sky cause such terror?

The airplane flew back a minute later and on the wings it said: COUNTY FAIR! ATTEND! RACING! FUN!

That's nothing to be afraid of, I thought.

I passed their room at nine-thirty and the door was open. On the walls I saw three calendars lined up with the date August 18, 2035, prominently circled.

"Good evening," I said pleasantly. "Say, you have a lot of nice calendars there. Come in mighty handy."

"Yes," they said.

I went on to my room and stood in the dark before turning on the light and wondered why they should need three calendars, all with the year 2035. It was crazy, but *they* were not. Everything about them was crazy except themselves, they were clean, rational people with beautiful faces, but it began to move in my mind, the calendars, the clocks, the wristwatches they wore, worth a thousand dollars each if I ever saw a wristwatch, and they, themselves, constantly looking at the time. I thought of the handkerchief that wouldn't burn and the seamless clothing, and the sentence "I've always hated Westercott."

I've always hated Westercott.

Lionel Westercott. There wouldn't be two people in the world with an unusual name like that. Lionel Westercott. I said it softly to myself in the summer night. It was a warm evening, with moths dancing softly, in velvet touches, on my screen. I slept fitfully, thinking of my comfortable job, this good little town, everything peaceful, everyone happy, and these two people in the next room, the only people in the town, in the world, it seemed, who were not happy. Their tired mouths haunted me. And sometimes the tired eyes, too tired for ones so young.

I must have slept a bit, for at two o'clock, as usual, I was wakened by her crying, but this time I heard her call out, "Where are we, where are we, how did we get here, where are we?" And his voice, "Hush, hush, now, please," and he soothed her.

"Are we safe, are we safe, are we safe?"

"Yes, yes, dear, yes."

And then the sobbing.

Perhaps I could have thought a lot of things. Most minds would turn to murder, fugitives from justice. My mind did not turn that way. Instead I lay in the dark, listening to her cry, and it broke my heart, it moved in my veins and my head and I was so unbearably touched by her sadness and loneliness that I got up and dressed and left the house. I walked down the street and before I knew it I was on the hill over the lake and there was the library, dark and immense, and I had my janitor's key in my hand. Without thinking why, I entered the big silent place at two in the morning and walked through the empty rooms and down the aisles, turning on a few lights. And then I got a couple of big books out and began tracing some paragraphs and lines down and down, page after page, for about an hour in the early, early dark morning. I drew up a chair and sat down. I fetched some more books. I sent my eye searching. I grew tired. But then at last my hand paused on a name, "William Westercott, politician, New York City. Married to Aimee Ralph on January 1998. One child, Lionel, born February 2000."

I shut the book and locked myself out of the library and walked home, cold, through the summer morning with the stars bright in the black sky.

I stood for a moment in front of the sleeping house with the empty porch and the curtains in every room fluttering with the warm August wind, and I held my cigar in my hand but did not light it. I listened, and there above me, like the cry of some night bird, was the sound of the lonely woman, crying. She had had another nightmare, and, I thought, nightmares are memory, they are based on things remembered, things remembered vividly and horridly and with too much detail, and she had had another of her nightmares and she was afraid.

I looked at the town all around me, the little houses, the houses with people in them, and the country beyond the houses, ten thousand miles of meadow and farm and river and lake, highways and hills and mountains and cities all sizes sleeping in the time before dawn, so quietly, and the streetlights going out now when there was no use for them at this nocturnal hour. And I thought of all the people in the whole land and the years to come, and all of us with good jobs and happy in this year.

Then I went upstairs past their door and went to bed and

listened and there, behind the wall, the woman was saying over and over again, "I'm afraid, I'm afraid," faintly, crying.

And lying there I was as cold as an ancient piece of ice placed between the blankets, and I was trembling, though I knew nothing, I knew everything, for now I knew where these travelers were from and what her nightmares were and what she was afraid of, and what they were running away from.

I figured it just before I went to sleep, with her crying faintly in my ears. Lionel Westercott, I thought, will be old enough to be president of the United States in the year 2035.

Somehow, I did not want the sun to rise in the morning.

HAIL TO THE CHIEF

2003–2004

"HOW'S THAT AGAIN?"

Silence.

"Would you mind repeating that?"

Silence and an up-and-down murmur on the phone.

"This is a bad line. I can't believe what I'm hearing! Go over that again."

The government official was rising slowly from his chair, the telephone crammed to his ear. He was staring out the window, then at the ceiling, and then at the walls. Slowly he sat down again.

"Now repeat that."

The phone made noises.

"Senator Hamfritt, you say? Just a moment. I'll call you right back."

The official hung up, turned in his chair, and stared out across the lawn at the White House.

Then he reached over and touched the intercom button.

When his secretary appeared at the door he said, "Sit down, you must hear this."

He picked up the phone, punched a number and the speakerphone.

When a voice came on he said, "This is Elliot. Did you call in the last few minutes? You did. Now, go over those details again. Senator Hamfritt, you say? An Indian casino? In North Dakota? Yes. How many senators? Thirteen? They were there last night? You sure of the facts? He wasn't drunk? He *was* drunk? Well, it's late, but I'll call the president."

The official put the phone down and slowly turned to his secretary.

"Do you know that idiot Hamfritt?"

She nodded.

"Do you know what that damn fool has done?"

"I can hardly wait."

"He went off a few hours ago to an Indian reservation in North Dakota with twelve senators. Said he was investigating affairs in the territory."

The secretary waited.

"He then engaged in a series of roulettes with the chief of

the largest tribe, Chief Iron Cloud. They put up New York City and lost that."

The secretary leaned forward.

"Then they started gambling with states—and lost! By two in the morning, drinking with the Indian chief, they managed to lose the entire United States of America."

"Holy shit," said the secretary.

"I might kill myself, but first, who's gonna call the White House and tell the president about this?"

"Not me," said the secretary.

THE PRESIDENT OF THE UNITED STATES ran across the airport tarmac.

"Mr. President!" an attaché cried. "You're not dressed!"

The president glanced down at the pajamas under his overcoat.

"I'll change on the plane. Where the hell are we going?"

The attaché turned to the pilot. "Where the hell are we going?"

The pilot glanced at a transcript and said, "The Pocahontas Big Red Casino, Ojibway, North Dakota."

"Where in hell is that?"

"On the Canadian border," said the attaché. "It's safe. Only the caribou vote there. Last year, a landslide."

"Is the airport large enough for Air Force One?" said the president.

"Barely."

"What time is it?"

"Three a.m."

"My God, the things we do to run a country," said the president.

On board, the president sat while drinks were poured and said, "Give me the details."

"Well, here's how it is, Mr. President. There was a meeting of Democratic senators in North Dakota. Thirteen of them went to the Pocahontas Big Red Casino for a night of whoopee."

"You can say that again," said the president of the United States.

"Well, one thing led to another and they wound up giving away the whole damned country."

"In one roll of the dice?"

"No, as I heard it, one state at a time."

"My God."

"To be accurate, sir, they lost New York *City* first, but the first *state* to go was Florida."

"That figures."

"After that it was most of the southern states. Something to do with the Civil War."

"How's that?"

"I don't know. It's still all a little fuzzy. But the Civil War's never been completely forgotten, and it would be just like southern Democrats to deal it back to the reds."

"Then what?"

"Well, state by state, ending with Arizona, and the next thing you know, with a final toss, America the Beautiful, sea to shining sea, belonged to Iron Cloud."

"The Indian chief?"

"Yes. He runs the casino."

The president mused and then said, "If they can drink, so can I. Refill my glass."

THE PRESIDENT OF THE UNITED STATES plunged into the Pocahontas Big Red Casino and glared around.

"Where's the smoke-filled room?"

The attaché pointed.

"And where are those stupid rotten damn fool senators?"

"In that room, naturally."

The president slammed the door wide to startle the thirteen senators, who stood staring at the floor.

"Sit down!" cried the president. "No, stand while I hit you! Now hear this. Are you all sober?"

They nodded.

"Then we *all* need a drink!"

Smith, the attaché, hurried out of the room. In moments, vodka was brought in.

"Okay, drink up and let's solve this mess."

He scowled at them and said, "My God, you make the Rolling Stones look like the Last Supper."

There was a long silence.

"Who's responsible? Senator Hamfat?"

"Hamfritt," murmured one of the senators.

"Hamfritt. Hold on. Smith, do the news media know about this?"

"Not yet, sir."

"My God, if the networks ever found out we'd be road-kill."

"There was a call from CNN an hour ago, wondering what's going on. . . ."

"Send someone to shoot them."

"We can't do that, Mr. President."

"Try."

The president turned back to the thirteen senators. "All right, tell me just how you managed to give away our purple mountain majesties and fruited plains."

"Not outright, the whole kit and caboodle," said one senator. "It happened piecemeal."

"Piecemeal!" shouted the president.

"We started slow and gained speed. We played poker at first, but got excited and moved on to blackjack, but then roulette seemed best."

"Roulette, sure. That way you lose everything fast."

"Fast," the senators agreed, nodding.

"Anyway, you know how it is when you're losing, you double your bets. So we doubled up and offered the Indians North and South Carolina, and by God, we lost them too.

Then we drank some more and got excited and offered them North and South Dakota, and lost!"

"Go on," said the president.

"Then we bet California."

"That was a *double* bet?"

"Yes, sir, California is really four states: north and south, Hollywood and L.A."

"Oh," said the president.

"Anyway, in a few hours we lost about everything and someone had the idea that maybe we should call Washington, DC."

"I'm glad you thought of that," said the president. "Smith, is any of this crud legally binding?"

"Only if you consider the reactions of France, Germany, Russia, Japan, and China, Mr. President."

"Okay. Are there any lawyers in this damn casino?"

"Sure," said the attaché. "Two hundred of 'em at poker upstairs. Shall I get one?"

"Are you nuts!?" said the president. "Within hours we'd be up to our chins."

The President sat for a long moment, his eyes closed, gripping his knees, white-knuckled, as if he were running blind into a mountain.

He wet his lips half a dozen times, but only when he clenched his knees tighter did the steam come out of his mouth in a hiss and sputter. "Of all the stupid, dim-bulb, half-wit, half-ass, crazy—"

"Yes, sir," one of the senators said.

"I'm not done!" the president cried.

"Yes, sir."

"Of all the damned silly, blind—"

The president stopped.

"Dim-bulb bastards," someone suggested.

"Rum-headed, bastard idiots!"

Everyone nodded.

"Maniac, lunatic, mindless, stupid jerks! Jesus God, God almighty!"

The president opened his eyes. "Do you realize that, in comparison, this will make the United Nations look like a gathering of angels? A congress of Einsteins! A full house of Fathers, Sons, and Holy Ghosts!"

Silence.

"Mr. President, sir, your face is very red."

"I thought," said the president, "it would be purple. Is there anything in the Constitution that would let the president beat up, kill, massacre, hang, electrocute, or draw and quarter these dumb-cluck senators?"

"Nothing in the Constitution, Mr. President," Smith said.

"At the next session of Congress, put it in."

At last he ceased and let his fists fall open. He stared at each empty paw to see if some answer lay there. Tears fell from his eyelashes.

"What're we gonna do?" he bleated. "What're we gonna do?"

"Mr. President."

"What're we gonna do?" he cried again, quietly.

"Sir."

The president looked up.

A Native American gentleman in a tall hat stood there. He was very short and resembled a squaw.

The short Native American gentleman said, "May I make a suggestion, sir? The Chief of the Iroquois Waukesha Chippewa Council and owner of this casino and now proprietor of the United States of America wonders if you would want an audience with him."

The president of the United States tried to rise.

"Don't get up." The short man in the tall black hat turned and opened the door and a great iron-eyed solemn shadow glided through.

This man drifted in on soft wild bobcat feet, a tall shadow within a shadow. He was not quite seven feet tall, and the look on his serene face was the look of Eternity; the stare of dead presidents and lost Indian braves now come alive in the precipice face of this new visitor.

Someone, perhaps the small squawlike pathfinder, seemed to be humming a celebratory tune under his breath, something about a chief, something about hailing.

A great voice of muted storms spoke on high from this owner of many casinos.

The small squawlike servant below translated.

"He asks, what seems to be the trouble here?"

At this there was a collective impulse in the senators to hurl themselves at the exit, but something froze them in place: the small sounds of veins popping in the brow of the president of the United States.

He massaged his head to calm his raging veins and gasped: "You have stolen our country."

The voice spoke above and was translated below.

"Just one state at a time."

From that great height, a murmur fell upon the small Indian, who nodded several times.

"He now proposes," said the small Indian, "one last game. The chief is willing to gamble like a good sport and maybe lose the country."

A trembling, as of a great earthquake, shook the senators. Smiles trembled on their lips. The president felt the need to faint but did not.

"One last game?" he moaned. "And if we lose again? What do we even have to offer?"

The small Indian chatted up along the length of great redwood flesh and an utterance responded.

"You give us France and Germany."

"We couldn't do that!" cried the president.

"Oh no?" said the great storm voice.

The president shrank two sizes within his suit.

"Also," the shadow moved like winter above.

"Also?" piped the suddenly former president of the United States.

"The rules," recited the small interpreter below. "If you

lose, we keep the United States and you build casinos in all fifty states plus grade schools, high schools, and colleges throughout the Indian territories. Yes?"

The president of the United States nodded.

"And if you win," the little man went on, "you get the states back, but the same things must happen: You build schools and casinos in all territories, even though you have won."

"Incredible!" the president cried. "You can't apply the same rules win *or* lose!"

Shadows whispered.

"That's the way the cookie crumbles."

The president swallowed and at last said, "Let's begin."

The great steam-shovel-size fingers of the owner of all fifty states' Big Red Casinos moved out on the air. There was a deck of cards vised in the thick fingers.

"Deal," a voice echoed in up-country.

The president found all of his limbs inert.

"Blackjack," whispered the small assistant Indian. "Two cards each."

At last, slowly, the president of the United States laid out the cards, facedown.

A voice rumbled above.

The little man said, "You first."

The president picked up the cards, and a great smile widened on his face. He tried in vain to control his smile but was unable to do so.

He looked up at the huge Indian chief and said, "Now yours."

Thunder sounded above.

The interpreter said, "First, let's see your hand."

The president of the United States turned his cards over. They totaled nineteen.

"Now you," whispered the president.

Thunder rolled again and the small Indian said, "You win."

"How can you tell?" said the president, "if you don't turn your cards over? Perhaps you have twenty, or twenty-one."

The weather changed high in the room and the little Indian said, "You win. The country is yours. But, one last small item."

He handed the president a piece of paper.

The paper was inscribed: *Twenty-six dollars and ninety cents.*

"That," said the small Indian, "is the same amount of money paid for Manhattan many moons ago."

The president took out his billfold.

A voice rumbled from on high.

"He says, small bills only," said the interpreter.

The president handed over the money and the redwood's huge hand reached out and took it.

Up toward the ceiling the voice rumbled again.

"What now?" asked the president.

The interpreter translated. "He says he hopes you will build many ships and he will come to the harbor to bid you farewell on your journey back to wherever you came from."

"He said that, did he?"

The president of the United States stared at the cards, still untouched, on the table.

"Don't I get to see, to make sure I haven't gypped you?"

The small Indian shook his head.

The president went to the door, turned, and said, "What's this about sailing? I'm not going anywhere."

A voice whispered from above.

"Oh no?"

And the president of the United States snuck out, followed by his senators.

WE'LL JUST ACT NATURAL

1948–1949

It was about seven in the evening. Susan kept getting up and looking out the porch window, down off the hill at the railroad tracks, the trains running in, the smoke rising. The red and green lights were reflected in her wide brown eyes. In the darkness, her plump hand was a darker darkness. She kept pressing her mouth and looking at the clock. "That old clock must be fast," she said. "That crazy old tin clock."

"Ain't no crazy clock," said Linda, in the corner, a stack of phonograph records in her black hands, scuffling them through. She picked one out, eyed it, put it on the Grafanola, and cranked the machine. "Why'nt you just sit down and un-worry yourself, Mom?"

"My feet is still in good shape," said Susan. "I'm not so old."

"He comin', he comin', that's all. An' if he ain't comin', he ain't," said Linda. "You can't push that train any faster or flop them signals up and down. What time he say he comin'?"

"Seven-fifteen he said the train was, here for half an hour, on his way to New York, and he'd stop, said he'd just take that taxi right here, said not to try to meet him at the station."

"He ashamed, that's why," sneered Linda.

"You shut up, or get on home!" said Susan at her daughter. "He's a good man. I worked for his family when he's no bigger'n my hand. Used to carry him downtown on my shoulder. He's not ashamed!"

"That's a long time ago, fifteen years; he's *big* now."

"He sent me his book, didn't he?" cried Susan indignantly. She reached out her hand to the worn chair and picked the book up and opened it and read from the inscription on the title page. "To my dear Mammy Susan, with all my love, from Richard Borden." She snapped the book shut. "There you are!"

"That don't mean nothin', that's just writin', anyone can write that."

"You heard what I said."

"He makes a hunerd thousan' dollars a year now, why he goin' to bother with you, come outa his way?"

" 'Cause I remembers his mother an' his father an' his grandma an' grandpa, 'cause I worked for all of 'em, thirty years I worked, that's why, an' him being a writer why wouldn' he wanta see me, an' talk about all that?"

"I don't know." Linda shook her head. "Don't ask me."

"He's comin' on that seven-fifteen train, you watch and see."

The Grafanola started to play the Knickerbocker Quartette singing "Pretty Baby."

"Shut that thing off," said Susan.

"I ain't botherin' nobody."

"I can't hear."

"You don't need your ears, you got eyes, you see him comin'."

Susan went over and flipped the switch. The voices died. The silence was sharp and heavy. "There," said Susan, looking at her daughter. "Now I can think."

"What you going to do to him when he come?" asked Linda, looking up, eyes white and sly.

"What you mean?" Susan was careful.

"You goin' to kiss him, hug him?"

"I don't know, I didn't think about that."

Linda laughed. "You better start thinkin'. He's a big boy now. He ain't no kid. Maybe he won't like being hugged and kissed."

"I'll do what I'll do when the time comes," replied Susan, turning away. A little frown formed on her brow. She felt like slapping Linda. "Stop puttin' ideas in my head. We'll just act natural, like always."

"I bet he just shakes hands and sits on the edge of his chair."

"He won't do that. He was always one to laugh."

"I bet he don't call you Mammy in person. Bet he calls you Mrs. Jones."

"He used to call me Aunt Jemima, said I looked just like her, always wanted me to fix his pancakes. He was the cutest little boy you ever seen."

"He's not bad now, from the pictures I seen."

Susan shut her eyes for a long moment and said nothing. Then she said, "You ought to have your mouth washed out with lye." She touched the window curtains, searching the land again, looking for the smoke on the horizon. Suddenly, she set up a cry. "There it is! There she comes! I knew it, I knew it!" She glanced wildly at the clock. "Right on time! Come look!"

"I seen a train before."

"There she comes, look at that smoke!"

"I seen smoke enough to last me all my life."

The train roared into the station below, with a clangor and a belling and a great burning sound.

"Won't be long now," said Susan, smiling, showing a gold tooth.

"Don't hold your breath."

"I feel too good, talk all you want; I feel *fine*!"

The train was stopped now, and people were getting out. She could see them, small, small, at the base of the hill, in the concrete station, moving and milling. She thought of him and what he looked like now and what he had been like then. She remembered the time when he had returned from school, when he was seven, and had missed saying good-bye to her. She lived at home in the outer part of town. Every night she took a trolley at four o'clock. And he had missed walking with her to the trolley. Crying, he had run down the street after her. And found her just in time and embraced her, sobbing against her legs while she reached down and petted and cooed over him.

"That's something *you* never done," said Susan, angrily.

"What didn't I do?" asked Linda, surprised.

"Never mind." Susan lapsed once more into her remembering. And then that time, when he was thirteen and had returned from two years in California and had found her in the kitchen of his grandmother's house and whirled her around, laughing and embracing her. She smiled with the thought. It was a good thought. And now, fifteen years after that, him a big Hollywood writer on his way to the opening of his play in New York. And in the mail six months ago his first published book, and yesterday the letter saying he would stop to see her. She hadn't slept very well last night.

"No white man's worth all this," said Linda. "I'm goin' home."

"You sit down," commanded Susan.

"I don't want to be here when he don't show up," said Linda. "I'll phone you later." She walked to the door and opened it.

"Come back here and sit down," said Susan. "He'll be here any minute."

Linda stood with the door half open. She shut it and waited a minute, leaning silently against it, shaking her head.

"There's a yellow cab comin' up the hill now," called Susan, bent to the cold windowpane. "I bet he's in it!"

"You'll be poor by mornin'."

They waited.

"Oh," said Susan, blinking.

"What?"

"That fool cab turned down the other way."

"I bet he's just sittin' down there in the lounge car, drinkin' a drink. I bet he's in with a bunch of other men an' can't get away, afraid to tell them what he wants to do in a small town, take a cab an' come up to see some colored woman friend of his."

"He ain't doin' that. He's in a taxi now. I *know*."

Ten minutes and then fifteen passed.

"He should be here by now," said Susan.

"He ain't."

"Maybe that ain't the train; maybe the clock's wrong."

"Want me to phone 'time' for you?"

"Get away from that phone!" cried Susan.

"All right, all right, I just *thought*."

"You just thought, you thought, get away!" She raised her hand and her face was twisted.

They waited once more. The clock ticked.

"You know what I'd do if I was you?" said Linda. "I'd go right down to that train an' get on an' say 'Where's Mr. Borden?' an' I'd hunt till I found him, an' there he'd be, I bet, with all his friends in the lounge car, drinkin', an' I'd walk up to him an' say, 'Looky here, Richard Borden, I knew you when you was all damp! You said you was comin' to see me! Why didn't you?' That's what I'd say, right in front of those men friends of his!"

Susan said nothing. It was seven thirty-five. In ten more minutes the train would be pulling out again. He's delayed, she thought. He has to come up. He's not that sort.

"Well, Mom, I'm goin' home. I'll phone later."

This time she did not try to stop Linda. The door shut. Her footsteps faded away down the hall.

With her away, Susan felt better. She felt that now with the evil influence of her child gone, Richard Borden must certainly arrive. He had just been *waiting* for Linda to leave, so they could be alone!

He's down there somewhere, she thought, on that train. Her heart sickened. What if he was in the club car now, drinking, as Linda said? No! Maybe he forgot, maybe he didn't even *know* this was his hometown! Some mistake, the porter's forgot to call, or something. She twisted her hands together. Sitting down there in the warm club car, drinking. Sitting down there in the nighttime after fifteen years. All the yellow bright lights on the train, the slow steam rising. Come on, Richard! You don't come, I'll tell your mama! Her breathing was deep and heavy. She felt very old. You don't come in a minute, I'll do what Linda said, come down an' speak right up to you!

No. She couldn't do that. Not embarrass him in front of his friends. Not that. Let him sit there, then. It was all a mistake, anyway. The clock was crazy.

The train gave a warning shriek.

No, she thought. They *can't* be getting ready to leave.

She saw the passengers climb back on the train. He must be sick, she thought. Not even on that train at all. Sick in Chicago, maybe. Sure. And if he *is* down there now, right *now*, did he get off, did he try and catch a cab at all? Maybe not enough cabs? Did he walk around the station or the town, or even look up here to the hill and the house where she was? Would she hear from him tomorrow, from New York? Or ever again, for that matter? No, never; that is, if he really was down there now. He'd never write again after this.

The train whistle blew again. A big funnel of steam rose up on the night air.

Then, with a jolting, the train moved out of the station, gained speed, and was gone.

Susan stood by the window. The house was silent. She looked at the western horizon. That must have been the wrong train. Another would be along in a minute. She picked up the alarm clock. It made a cheap tinny clicking in her hand. "Crazy old clock, givin' the wrong time!" she cried and dropped it into the wastebasket.

She went back to the window.

The phone rang once. She didn't turn. The phone rang again, insistently. She still watched the horizon. The phone rang six more times and would not stop.

Finally she turned and went to pick it up. She held it in her hands for a time before lifting the receiver. Then she put the receiver to her ear.

"Hello, Mom?"

It was Linda.

"Mom, you come over to my place for the night. I know how you feel," said the voice.

"What do you mean?" cried Susan, angrily, into the mouthpiece. "He was just here!"

"What?"

"Yes, an' he was tall an' good lookin', an' he came in a yellow cab just for a minute, an' you know what I done? I hugged an' kissed him an' danced him around!"

"Oh, Mom!"

"An' he talked an' laughed an' was good to me an' gave me a ten-dollar bill, an' we remembered old times, everybody, everything, that's what happened, an' he went back in his yellow cab an' caught that train an' it's gone. He's a real gentleman!"

"Mom, I'm so glad."

"Yes, sir," said Susan, looking out the window, holding the phone in her shaking hands. "A real *gentleman*!"

Olé, Orozco! Siqu*e*iros, *Sí*!

2003–2004

Sam Walter burst into my office, stared around at all the collectors' posters on the wall, and said: "Whatta you know about the major artists of Mexico?"

"Rivera," I said. "Martinez. Delgado."

"How about this?"

Sam tossed a bright folder on my desk.

"Read it!"

I read what I saw in big red letters.

"Siqueiros, *sí*, Orozco, *olé*." I read further. "Gambit Gallery. Boyle Heights. They're having an Orozco Siqueiros art show across the river?"

"Read the small print." Sam tapped the brochure.

"A memorial exhibit of the fine work of Sebastian Rodriguez, heir to the throne of Siqueiros and Orozco."

"I'm taking you," Sam said. "Look at the date."

"April twentieth. Hell, that's today, two p.m. Hell, that's in an hour! I can't—"

"You can. You're an art gallery expert, right? It's not an opening, it's a closing. A funeral."

"Funeral?!"

"The artist, Sebastian Rodriguez, will attend, but dead."

"You mean—?"

"It's a wake. His mom and dad will be there. His brothers and sisters will come. Cardinal Mahoney will drop by."

"Good Lord, the artist was that good? All those people!"

"It was supposed to be a party, but he died in a fall. So instead of canceling, they fetched the body. Now it's a semi-mass, with candles and choirs in lace."

"Jesus!" I said.

"You can say that again."

"Jesus. A funeral mass for an unknown artist in a fourth-rate gallery in Mexican-Hispanic-Jewish Boyle Heights?"

"Turn the pages. The ghosts of Orozco and Siqueiros are there."

I turned the pages and gasped.

"Holy mackerel!"

"You can say that again," said Sam.

On the freeway heading to Jewish-Hispanic Boyle Heights I gibbered.

"This guy's a genius! How did you find him?"

"The police," said Sam, driving.

"The *what*?"

"Cops. He was a criminal. A few hours in jail."

"Hours? What had he done?"

"Big stuff. Mind-blowing. But no reason to be stuffed in the slammer. Big in one way, small in another. Look up!"

I looked up.

"See that overhead?"

"The bridge? Now it's behind us! Why—?"

"That's where he fell."

"Jumped?"

"No, fell." Sam speeded up. "Notice anything else?"

"About what?"

"The overhead. The bridge."

"What was I supposed to notice? You went too fast."

"We'll come back later. You'll see."

"Where he died?"

"Where he had his finest hour. *Then* died."

"Where he was Orozco, Siqueiros's ghosts?"

"You got it!"

Sam wheeled off the freeway.

"We're here!"

IT WAS NOT AN ART GALLERY.

It was a church.

There were bright pictures on all the walls, each so stunning in their brilliance they seemed to leap on the air in flames. But other flames intervened. Two or three hundred candles flared in a great circle around the vast gallery. They had been lit for hours, and their flames made it high summer, so you forgot you had just come in from April.

The artist was there but concerned with his new occupation, an eternity to be filled with silence.

He was not fixed in a coffin but laid out on a cloud embankment of snow-white cloth, which seemed to drift him up through the constellations of candles that now trembled in a draft from a side door where a member of the clergy had just entered.

I recognized the face immediately. Carlos Jesus Montoya, keeper of a great sheepfold of Latinos overlapping the dry bed of the empty Los Angeles River. Priest, poet, adventurer in rain forests, love assassin of ten thousand women, headliner, mystic, and now critic for *Art News Quarterly*, he stood as on the prow of a craft sinking in flames to survey the walls where Sebastian Rodriguez's lost dreams were suspended.

I looked where he looked and sucked air.

"What?" Sam whispered.

"These paintings," I said, my voice rising, "are not paintings. They're color photographs!"

"Sh!" someone shhed.

"Pipe down," Sam whispered.

"But—"

"It was all planned." Sam glanced around nervously. "First the photos to pique the viewers' curiosity. Then the real paintings. A double art premiere."

"Still," I said. "For photos, they're brilliant!"

"Sh," someone shhed even louder.

The great Montoya was staring at me from across a sea of summer fire.

"Brilliant photos," I whispered.

Montoya read my lips and nodded with majesty, like a torero on a Seville afternoon.

"Hold on!" I said, almost grasping something. "Those pictures. I've seen them somewhere else!"

Carlos Jesus Montoya refixed his stare at the walls.

"Come on," hissed Sam and pulled me toward the door.

"Wait!" I said. "Don't break my chain of thought."

"Idiot," Sam almost cried, "you'll get yourself killed."

Montoya read his lips too and nodded the merest of nods.

"Why would someone want to kill me?" I said.

"You know too much!"

"I know nothing!"

"You do! *Andale!* Vamoose!"

And we were out the door from hot burning summer to cold April, but were thrust aside by a cloud of weeping followed by the weepers, a dark mass of women shawled in black and shedding fountains.

"No family weeps that hard," said Sam. "Former lovers."

I listened.

"Sure," I said.

More crying followed. More women, larger and plumper, followed by a solemn gent as courtly and quiet as guidon spears.

"Family," Sam said.

"We're not leaving so soon?"

"There's a crisis. I wanted you to see everything so you would take it in like a virgin observer, nonjudgmental, before you latched onto the reality."

"How much you charge for that bag of manure you just filled?"

"No manure. Just artists' blood, artists' dreams, and critics' judgments to be won and lost."

"Give me that bag. I'll fill it for you."

"No. Step back in. Take one last look at genius slain and truth about to be corrupted."

"You only talk this way late Saturdays with your clothes on and the bottle empty."

"It's not Saturday. Here's my flask. Drink. One last swallow, one last stare."

I drank and stood in the door where the harvest weather breathed out smelling of hot candle wax.

Far away calm Sebastian drifted on his white cloth boat. Far off some boy choirs chirped.

ON THE FREEWAY, speeding, I guessed.

"I know where we're going!"

"Shh," said Sam.

"To where Sebastian Rodriguez jumped."

"Fell!"

"*Fell* to his death."

"Look sharp. We're almost there."

"We are! Slow down. Ohmigod. There they *are*!"

Sam slowed down.

"Pull over," I said. "God, I must be out of my mind. Look."

"I *am*!"

On the freeway overpass bridge there indeed they were.

"Sebastian's paintings on the gallery walls!"

"Those were photos. These are real."

And indeed they were, brighter, bigger, phenomenal, mind-blowing, cataclysmic.

"Graffiti," I said at last.

"But *what* graffiti," Sam said, gazing up as at a cathedral's stained glass.

"Why didn't you show me these first?"

"You did see them, but with peripheral vision at sixty miles per hour. Now you've got them twenty-twenty."

"But why now?"

"I didn't want the real to interfere with the crazy mystery. I wanted to give you answers so you could imagine all the lunatic questions."

"The photos in the gallery, the graffiti up there on the overhang. Which came first, the chicken or the egg?"

"Half chicken, half egg. The priest Montoya sped under these miracles a month ago, did a shocked double take, and almost braked himself into a road wreck."

"He was the first art collector of Sebastian's freeway annunciations and holy revelations?" I guessed.

"Right on! Staring at these Latino-American beauties he spun and ran back for a camera. The resulting blowups were so mind blasting, so eye and soul riveting, Montoya conceived a super master plan. Since most people would snub any freeway graffiti art, why not nail Sebastian's white-hot bouquets on the gallery walls to burn people's eyes and inflame their purses? Then, when it was too late to renege, change their minds and ask for their money back, stage the big revelation: 'If you think these gallery eye-winkers are God-given,' Montoya cried, 'fix your eyes on Freeway 101, overpass 89.' So Montoya hung these windows on burning life as photos and prepared to spring the truth on the critics when they were all safely on board. The problem was—"

"Sebastian fell on the freeway before the show could open?"

"Fell and endangered his reputation."

"I thought death improved an artist's chances for celebrity."

"Some, yes, some, no. Sebastian's was a special case. Complicated. When Sebastian fell—"

"How come he fell?"

"He was hanging upside down over the edge of the freeway overhang, painting, a pal holding his legs, when the pal sneezed, God yes, sneezed and let go."

"Jesus!"

"Nobody wanted to tell his folks or anyone the truth. Christ! Upside down painting illegal graffiti and crashing down in traffic. It was listed as a bike accident, though no bike was found. They washed the guilty paint off his hands before the coroner came. Which left Montoya—"

"With a gallery full of useless photo art."

"No! A gallery full of priceless relics from an artful dodger's life, dead too soon but thank God the inspired photos stayed to be bid for in prices that skyrocketed! Cardinal Mahoney added his imprimatur, and they shot through the ceiling."

"So no one ever told where the original artwork could be found?"

"No one ever will. The relatives warned their boy never to play on the freeway, and look what's happened! They might have survived a living festival where Sebastian was celebrated for the gallery photo stuff but, my God, look, it's overhang 89 on Freeway 101, but with him dead, it was too melancholy and too commercial. Then Montoya thought to light a thousand candles and create the Saint Sebastian church."

"How many people know this story?"

"Montoya, the gallery owner, maybe one or two aunts or uncles. Now you and me. Nobody will let the cat out of the bag to cross the freeway. Mum's the word. Reach over in the backseat. Feel around. What do you feel?"

I reached back, blind-handed.

"Feels like three buckets."

"What else?"

I probed. "A big paintbrush!"

"So?"

"Three buckets of paint!"

"Right!"

"For what?"

"To paint over Sebastian Rodriguez's freeway masterpiece graffiti."

"Paint over all those priceless murals, why?"

"If we leave them there, eventually someone will notice, compare them to the gallery photos, and the jig's up!"

"The world will discover he was only a freeway graffiti stuntman?"

"Or the world will spy his genius and gawkers will cause collisions or block traffic. Either way it's a no-go."

I stared up at the bright overhang.

"And who's gonna paint over the murals?"

"Me!" Sam said.

"How will you do it?"

"You'll hold me upside down, by my knees, while I whitewash. But blow your nose first. No sneezing."

"Siqueiros, nada, Orozco, no?"

"You can say that again."

I said it three times. Quietly.

THE HOUSE

1947

IT WAS AN INCREDIBLE, insane old house looking wildly out over the city with staring eyes. Birds had built nests in its high cupolas so that the place resembled nothing more than a thin, night-haunted old woman, hair untidily kept.

They had walked up the long hill in the windy autumn night, Maggie and William, and now when she saw the house she set her Saks Fifth Avenue suitcase down and said, "Oh, *no*."

"Oh, yes." He carried his battered old luggage buoyantly. "Isn't it a bean? Look at her, isn't she priceless!"

"You paid two thousand dollars for *that*?" she cried.

"Why, it cost thirty thousand dollars, fifty years ago," he declared, proudly. "And it's all ours. Boy!"

She waited for her heart to beat again. She was sick. She looked at him and then at the house. "It—it looks a little like a Charles Addams house, doesn't it? You know, the man who draws the vampire cartoons for *The New Yorker*?"

But he was already up the walk. She came carefully after him up the moaning front steps. The house soared up, three mansarded, pillared, fluted, rococo flights of it, towers and peaks and bay windows pregnant with broken glass; a fine nicotine stain of years upon it. Inside there was a silence of moths and hung window shades and furniture draped like little white tombs.

Again she felt everything sink within her. When you have lived in a big clean house on a big secluded street all of your life, with servants invisibly keeping the order, with a phone wherever you put out your hand, with a bathtub big as a swimming pool, and your only exercise is the energy it takes to lift an immensely heavy dry martini, then what is one to think when confronted by a rusty mountain, a haunted catacomb, a thing of gray work and utter chaos? Oh God, she thought, if Americans' lives come to this, fewer houses, incredible prices. Why did people marry at all?

It was hard to keep her face together, to make it look right, because William was shouting up and down stairs, walking swiftly, tall, through the rooms, proud as if he'd built it himself.

"I am Hamlet's father's ghost," said William, coming down the dim stairs.

"—father's ghost," said an echo from up the stairwell, at the top of the house.

William smiled and pointed up. "Hear that? That's the Listener at the top of the house. Old friend of mine. He hears everything you say. I was saying to him only yesterday, *I love Maggie!*"

"I love Maggie," said the Listener at the top of the house.

"A man of taste, that Listener," said Bill. He came and held Maggie's shoulders. "Isn't this house *swell*?"

"It's big, I'll give you that. And it's dirty, I'll give you that. And it most certainly *is* old."

She watched his face watching hers. And by the slow change of his face she knew that her own face wasn't doing a very good job of loving the vast place. She had ripped her nylon stockings on a nail, coming in the door. There was dirt on the expensive tweed skirt she had brought from 'Frisco already, and—

He took his hands from her shoulders. He looked at her mouth. "You don't much care for it, do you?"

"Oh, it's not that—"

"Maybe we should have bought that trailer."

"Oh, no, don't be silly. It's just I have to get used to this. Who'd want to live in a bread box trailer? There's more *room* here."

"Or maybe waited another year to get married, with more money."

"Perhaps we won't have to stay here long, anyway," she

said, trying to be gay. But it was the wrong thing to say. He didn't want to go, ever. This was a place he loved and wanted to fix over. There was a permanence in the way he looked at it.

"Up here is the bedroom." At the top of the first landing, where a feeble bulb burned, he opened a door. There was a room with a four-poster bed in it. He had scrubbed and swept the room himself and fixed the bed as a surprise for her. There were bright pictures on the wall and new fresh yellow-print wallpaper.

"It's nice," she said, still forcing it.

He did not look at her as he said, tonelessly, "I'm glad you like it."

THE NEXT MORNING he was all through the house, up and down the stairs, whistling and singing, full of breakfast vigor and ideas. She heard him ripping down the old shades, sweeping the hall, breaking the old glass shards from a broken kitchen window. She lay in bed. The warm yellow sun streamed in the south window and touched her idle hand on the coverlet. She lay, not wanting to move, incredulous at the sound of her resilient husband ricocheting from room to room with the momentum of his inspiration. *Resilient* was the word. You hurt or disappointed him one day, and the next day it was forgotten. He bounced back. That was more than she could say for herself. He was like a string of firecrackers set off to explode all through the echoing house.

She slid from the bed. Let's try and make it better, she thought. Let's keep the face right. She looked in the mirror. Is there any way, she wondered, to *paint* a smile on?

He handed her a dust mop and a kiss after the instantaneous burnt breakfast.

"Onward, upward, excelsior!" he cried. "Do you realize that man's preoccupation is not with love or sex or getting on or keeping up with the Joneses? It is not for fame or fortune! No, man's longest battle, mistress, is with the element of dust. It comes in every joint and elbow of the house! Why, if we sat down and rocked in our rocking chairs for a year we'd be buried in dust, the cities would be lost, the gardens would be deserts, the living rooms dustbins! Christ, I wish we could pick the whole house up and shake it out!"

They worked.

But she tired. First it was her back and then it was, "My head aches." He brought her aspirin. And then it was sheer exhaustion from the many many rooms. She had lost count of the rooms. And the particles of dust in the rooms? God, it ran into the billions! She went sneezing and running her small nose into a hankie, confused and bitter-red, all through the house.

"You'd better sit down," he said.

"No, I'm all right," she said.

"You'd better go rest." He wasn't smiling.

"I'll be fine. It's not lunchtime yet."

That was the trouble. The first morning, and herself tired already. And she felt a rush of guilty color to her cheeks. Because it was a strange tiredness made of unnecessary strains and superfluous actions and tensions. You can only deceive yourself so far, no further. She was tired, yes, but not of the work, only of this place. Not twenty hours new in it, and already tired of it, sick of it. And he saw her sickness. One small part of her face showed it. Which part she could not tell. It was like a puncture in a tube, you couldn't tell where the puncture was until you submerged the tube and then bubbles rose in the water. She didn't want him to know her sickness. But every time she thought of her friends coming to see her and what they would say to one another at their private teas: "Whatever happened to Maggie Clinton?" "Oh, didn't you hear? She married that writer fellow and they live on Bunker Hill. On Bunker Hill, can you imagine? In an old haunted house or some such!" "We must go up some time." "Oh, yes, it's priceless. The thing is toppling over, simply toppling. Poor Mag!"

"You used to be able to play I-don't-know-how-many tennis sets every morning and afternoon, with a round of golf thrown in," he said.

"I'll be all right," she said, knowing nothing else to say.

They were on the landing. The morning sun fell through the tinted rim glasses of the high window. There were little pink glasses and blue glasses and red and yellow and purple and orange glasses. The many colors glowed on her arms and on the banister.

He had been staring for some moments at the little colored windowpanes. Now he looked at her. "Pardon the melodramatics," he said. "But I learned something when I was a kid, pretty young. My grandmother had a hall and at the top of the stairs was a window with little colored glass in it, just like this. I used to go up and look through the colored panes, and—" He tossed down the dust rag. "It's no use. You wouldn't understand." He walked down the stairs away from her.

She stood looking after him. She looked at the colored panes. What had he been trying to say, some ridiculous, obvious thing he had decided finally not to say? She moved to the window.

Through the pink pane the world was roseate below, and warm. The neighborhood, poised like a squalorous avalanche on the brink of a cliff, took on tones of the rose and a sunset.

She looked through a yellow pane. And the world was the sun, all bright and luminous and fresh.

She looked through a purple glass. The world was covered with cloud, the world was infected and sick, and people moving in that world were leprous, lost, and abandoned. The houses were black and monstrous. Everything seemed bruised.

She returned to the yellow pane. The sun was back. The smallest dog looked clever and bright. The dirtiest child looked washed. The rusty houses were seemingly painted afresh.

She looked down the stairs at where William was dialing

the phone, quietly, no expression on his face. And then she looked at the colored panes again and knew what he meant. You had a choice of panes to look through. The dark one or the light one.

She felt quite lost. She felt it was too late. Even when it isn't too late, sometimes you feel it is. To say something, to speak a word. One word. But she wasn't ready. The whole idea was too new to her. She couldn't speak now and fully mean it. It would have to seep into her. She could feel the first faint excitement, but then smothered with fear and hatred of herself. And then quick little thrusts of hate at the house and William, because they had made her hate herself. But finally it resolved into simple irritation, and only at her own blindness.

William was phoning below. His voice came up the bright stairwell. He was calling the real estate agent.

"Mr. Woolf? About that house you sold me last week. Look, do you think *I* could sell it? With maybe a *little* profit?"

There was a silence. She heard her heart beating swiftly.

William lay the phone down. He did not look up at her.

"He can sell it," William said. "For a little profit."

"For a little profit," said the Listener at the top of the house.

THEY WERE HAVING A SILENT LUNCHEON when somebody banged on the front door. William, with a silence unusual to him, went to answer.

"The darn doorbell doesn't work!" cried a woman's voice in the hall.

"Bess!" cried William.

"Bill, you old son of a—hey, this is a swell place!"

"Do you like it?"

"Do I *like* it? Tie a bandanna on my hairdo and hand me a mop!"

They jabbered on. Maggie, in the kitchen, put down her butter knife and listened, cold and apprehensive.

"God, what I wouldn't give for a place like this!" cried Bess Alderdice, stamping about the house. "Look at the hand-carved banister. Hey-soose; as the Spanish say; look at that crystal chandelier! Who'd you hit over the head, Bill?"

"We were lucky it was for sale," said Bill, in the hall.

"I've had my eye on this place for years! And you, you lucky bun-of-a-sitch, you grab it out from under sweet Bess Alderdice's grimy little claws."

"Bring your grimy little claws out into the kitchen and have some lunch."

"Lunch, hell, when do we work? I want a hand in this!"

Maggie appeared in the hall.

"Maggie!" Bess Alderdice in her tailored gabardines and flat-heeled shoes and wild black hair shouted at her. "How I *envy* you!"

"Hello, Bess."

"Girl, you look tired, or something," cried Bess. "Look,

you sit down and I'll help Bill. I've got muscles from eating Wheaties!"

"We're not going to stay here," said Bill quietly.

"You're what?" Bess looked at him as if he was insane. "In again out again, what's your name? Finnegan? Well, sell it to mama, mama wants it."

"We're going to try to find a small cottage somewhere," said Bill, falsely hearty.

"You know what you can do with cottages," said Bess, snorting. "Well, look here, since I'm going to buy this house out from under you, Bill, you can at least help me clean up *my* place! Give me a hand with these shades!" And she walked in to tear the moth-eaten shades off the parlor windows.

They worked all that afternoon, Bess and William. "You just go lie down, honey," said Bess, patting Maggie. "I'm getting free help."

The house thundered with echoes and scrapings. There were explosions of laughter. There were monster dust storms raging in the halls, and once Bess almost fell downstairs in her laughing. There was a banging and a creaking of nails drawn from walls, there was a musical tinkling of bumped chandeliers, there was the rip of old wallpaper coming off. "We'll make this into a tea room, and this here, why, we'll knock this wall out!" shouted Bess in the dust storms. "Right!" laughed William. "And I saw a reasonably priced set of antique chairs would just go in here!" said Bess. "Good idea!" said Bill. They gibbered and walked around, their hands on everything. He made blue chalk marks and threw useless furniture out windows, and banged the plumbing. "That's my boy!" cried Bess. "How about having a rack of fine Bavarian plates around this wall, Bill?" "Great! Wonderful!"

Maggie was outside of it. First she went uselessly up to her bedroom, then she walked down and out into the sunlight. But she couldn't escape the sound of Bill's happiness. He was planning and pounding and laughing, and all with another woman. He had forgotten about selling the house. What would he do later, when he remembered that he had called the real estate agent? Stop laughing, of course.

Maggie tightened her hands together. What was it that this Bess Alderdice had? Certainly not her breastless, hard, clumsy body, nor the wild unshorn locks of hair or unplucked brows! Whatever it was it was an enthusiasm and freshness and power that she, Maggie, did not have. But *might* have? After all, what right did Bess have coming here? It wasn't *her* house, was it? Not yet, anyway.

She heard Bess's voice through an open window. "Do you realize what a history this house has? It was built in 1899 by that lawyer. This used to be *the* neighborhood. This house had and still *has* dignity. People were proud to live here. They can *still* be."

Maggie stood in the hall. How did you make things right in the world? Things had been wrong until Bess walked in, righting them. How? Not with words. Words could not really make things one way or another. There was more than that. There were actions, continuous, going-on actions. Right now, Bill enjoyed Bess more than he would enjoy Maggie the rest of the day. Why? Because Bess did things with quick hands and an alive face, finished them, and went on to others.

Most of all, though, it was Bill. Had he ever worked in *his* life, nailed a nail, carried a carpet? No. Being a writer he had sat and sat and sat all his life until today. He was no more prepared for this House of Horror—step up, only a dime, one tenth of a dollar!—than she was. How then could he change suddenly overnight, fling himself on this house tooth and nail? The answer started with its simplicity. He loved Maggie. This would be her house. He'd have done the same if they stayed in an overnight cave. *Anywhere* was good, if Maggie was there.

Maggie closed her eyes. It all revolved around herself. *She* was the catalyst. Without her, he'd sit down, never work at all. And she'd been half gone all day. The secret lay not in Bess or William, but in love itself. Love was always the reason for work, for enthusiasm. And if William worked to make her happy, then couldn't she do the same for him? Love has always been building something somewhere. Either that or it decays. All married life you build—build egos, build houses, build children. If one stops, the other keeps going from the momentum. But then it's only a half structure. It roars down, finally, like a tower of cards.

Maggie looked at her hands. An apology now to Bill would be embarrassing, and superfluous. How to make things right, then? The same way you made them wrong. The same process, reversed. Things were wrong when you shattered a vase, ripped a drape, or left a book in the rain. You righted them by mending the vase, sewing the drape, buying a new book. These were *done* things. Her failure to this house was a history of things undone, the slow hand, the unwilling eyes, the lifeless voice.

She picked up a dust rag, climbed the stepladder, shined the chandelier; then she swept the halls with a great idea filling her. She saw the house, finished. Clean antiques, plush and warm color. New copper, shined woodwork, clean chandeliers, fresh-cut rose carpets, the upright piano rewaxed, the old oil lamps circuited with lights, the hand-carved banister re-stained, and the sun pouring though the high colored windows. It would be another age. Friends would dance in the wide ballroom on the third floor, under the eight huge chandeliers. There would be old music boxes, old wine, and a mellow warmth through the house like a fine sherry aroma. It would take time, they had little money, but in a year perhaps—

People would say, "It's wonderful at Bill and Mag's, like another age; so comfortable. You'd never guess from outside. I wish *we* could live on Bunker Hill in one of those wondrous old mansions!"

She ripped off great faded hunks of wallpaper. It was only then that Bill heard her and came to the hall door, surprised. "I *thought* I heard a noise. How long've *you* been working?"

"The last half hour." This time her smile was whole.

THE JOHN WILKES BOOTH/WARNER BROTHERS/MGM/NBC FUNERAL TRAIN

2003

I WAS JUST SETTLING DOWN for a long afternoon nap when Marty Felber burst into my office.

"My God!" he cried. "You've gotta come see!"

I lay back, easily. "See what?" I said.

Marty looked as if he might tear out his hair. "Haven't you heard? Down at the station, a special train is pulling in from Washington, DC. It's a steam engine, dammit, that boils water to drive the wheels. We haven't had a steam engine here for fifty years!"

"I've *seen* steam engines."

"No, no, this is strange. All black and covered with crepe."

"Covered with crepe? Let's get the hell out."

We got the hell out.

At the station we stared down the empty track. Far away we heard a melancholy wail, and above the horizon a cloud of steam rose to blow away in a sound of weeping.

The dark train glided from the twilight shadows in a drizzle of cold rain.

"Are there passengers?" I said.

"People crying. Hear?"

"My God, yes. Stand back."

The black train drifted like a dark cloud with the rain following and a ghostly steam clothing it.

The engine continued to exhale ghosts of smoke while it pulled a melancholy procession of cars, all burnt coal midnight black, with gardens of crepe papered along the roofs where the pale steam whispered and the weeping persisted from within the carriages.

On the side of one car was printed MGM.

On the second I read WARNER BROTHERS.

On the third and fourth, PARAMOUNT and RKO.

On the fifth, NBC.

A terrible cold filled my body. I stood, riven.

But finally, with Marty, I moved along the passing cars.

The black crepe rooftops stirred and the windows of each car seemed washed by rain.

The mournful cries from the engine sounded again and again as we moved swiftly, and the windows wept ceaselessly.

At last we arrived at the final, most melancholy car, where we stood staring through a great window dripping with rain.

Inside lay a long midnight coffin embedded in white flowers.

I stood as if struck by lightning, my heart gripped by a terrible fist. "Jesus!" I cried. "Nightmare! In my grandma's big picture book there was a train like this, but no names on the sides like MGM or Paramount." I stopped, for I could hardly breathe.

"Lord," I gasped. "In that window, the coffin. He's in there. Oh God, it's him!"

I shut my eyes.

"This is Abraham Lincoln's funeral train!"

From somewhere along the midnight train came another low cry. The black crepe fluttered.

Then a man came running and jolting down the platform, an old friend, Elmer Green, a studio press agent. He collided with me and yelled in my face.

"Hey, ain't this a catch? I'll give you the tour. Come on."

But I stood with my shoes sunk in concrete.

"What's wrong?" Green said.

"What's it look like?"

"You're not crying?" he said. "Cut that out. Let's go."

He backed off by the midnight cars, and Marty and I followed. I stumbled, my eyes blind with tears.

He stopped at last and said, "See that big red Pacific Electric trolley? Don't fit in with the rest of the train, right? Look. Middle window."

"Four guys in business suits, playing cards, smoking cigars. The plump guy, wait."

"Who?"

"Louis B. Mayer, the MGM studio mogul. Louie the Lion! Why's he here? He's dead."

"Not so you would notice. Okay. Back in 1930 Louis B. and his yes-men climbed on this big red trolley and pulled out of MGM Studios on its own track and trained to Glendale for surprise screenings. Then they piled back on this super Lionel electric train and roared home, shouting the good preview cards or letting them fly like confetti if they were bad."

"So?" I said, bleakly.

"So, when you've got trains like that and someone comes along with trains like this, you listen. Now climb aboard and meet Louis B., the reborn Christian Jewish Arab in this big trapped butterfly time machine."

I stared at my legs with half-blind eyes.

"Christ!" said Green. "Help me get him up."

Marty grabbed one elbow and Green the other and they yanked me up on the train.

We staggered through smoke-filled cars where scores of men riffled cards.

"God!" I exclaimed. "Is that Darryl Zanuck, 20th Century Fox's chief? And there, Harry Cohn, the beast of Gower Street? How in hell did they get lost in this nightmare?"

"Like I said, trapped in a time retrieval Butterfly Net. The biggest damned net in history scooped them out of the grave, with an offer they couldn't refuse: six feet of dirt, or a ticket on the John Wilkes Booth Forever Express."

"My God!"

"No, Elmo Wills," cried Green. "In an MGM Las Vegas basement, he jiggered some digital computers into conniption fits and nailed together a super-traveling catcher's mitt."

I stared along a smoke-filled gambling hall.

"Is that how you catch a train nowadays?"

"Yup," said Green.

"There are names of studios on each car," I said. "And inside, dead moguls, alive."

"They all invested in the virtual Net and Elmo, who said, 'What's the greatest locomotive in history? The train that brought Bobby Kennedy or Roosevelt home? What train toured the land, with everyone weeping, a century ago?' "

I felt the wetness on my cheek.

"A funeral train," I said, quietly. "Abe Lincoln's."

"Give the man a cigar."

The train jerked.

"Is it leaving?!" I cried. "I don't want to be seen on this abomination."

"Stay," said Green. "Name your salary."

I almost struck his smile.

"Damn you!"

"I already am." Green laughed. "But I'll recover."

The train jerked again with grinding sounds.

My friend Marty dashed ahead and came running back.

"You gotta see! The next car is jammed full of lawyers."

"Lawyers?" I turned to Green.

"They're suing," said Green. "Schedule problems. Which towns do we visit? Which broadcasts do we do? Which book contracts do we sign? Do we go with NBC or CNN? That sort."

"That sort!" I cried and plunged ahead, with Marty in full pursuit.

We ran through mobs of lunatics who were all yelling, pointing, and cursing.

At the fourth car I flung the door wide upon a midnight meadow of firefly light; all dancing sparks of blind machines.

Everywhere I saw cosmic banks of fire and spectral shapes of digital illumination.

This dim cave was lit by what seemed a rocket ship control panel; a man, not quite a dwarf, spidered his fingers quickly in patterns over the board. It was, indeed, the inventor of the incredible, blasphemous Butterfly Harvester.

I raised my hands in fists and the dwarf exclaimed, "You must hit me, yes?"

"Hit, no. Kill. What have you *done*?"

"Done?" cried the man. "I've mouth-to-mouth-breathed history. I might hurl my Net to trap Ben Hur's chariot or Cleopatra's barge and cry havoc and let loose the dogs of time."

He stared down and stroked his hands over the bright configurations, watching the lost years, talking half to himself.

"You know, I often thought if there'd been a fire at Ford's Theatre earlier that night in 1865, this funeral train would have been lost and the history of America changed forever."

"Say again?" I said.

"Fire," Elmo repeated. "At Ford's Theatre."

"Fire," I whispered, then thought: you never yell "fire" in a crowded theater. But what if you yell it on a crowded theater *train*?

Suddenly I was shrieking.

"Sons of bitches!"

I leaped to the back car door and flung it open wide.

"Bastards!"

Three dozen lawyers jumped at my steam-whistle shriek.

"Fire!" I screamed. "Ford's Theatre is on fire! Fire!" I shrieked.

And everyone on the damned and terrible train heard.

Old-fashioned doors were flung wide. Old-fashioned windows flew up, jam-packed with yells.

"Hold on!" cried Green.

"No!" I shouted. "Fire, fire!"

I ran, yelling, through car after car and spread the blaze.

"Fire!"

And panic suctioned all and everyone off the train.

The platform swarmed with victims and crazed lawyers, scribbling names and babbling.

"Fire," I whispered a final time, and the train was as empty as a dentist's office on a bad noon.

Green staggered up to me, and this time his feet looked sunk in concrete. His face was ashen and he seemed unable to breathe.

"Turn the train around," I said.

"What?"

Marty led me through a litter of unlit Cuban cigars and playing cards.

"Around," I wept. "Take the train back to Washington Station, 1865, April."

"We can't."

"You just *came* from there. Back, oh dear God, back."

"No return tickets. We can only go ahead."

"Ahead? Does MGM still have a track switch not covered up by asphalt? Pull in there, like in 1932, drop Louis B. Mayer, tell him Thalberg's alive on the fourth car back, Mayer will have a heart attack."

"Louie B.?"

"Harry Cohn too," I said.

"MGM's not his studio."

"He can call a cab or hitch a ride, but no one gets back on this stupid idiot bastard train."

"No one?"

"Unless they want to be buried in Ford's Theatre when I really strike a match and light the fire."

The lawyer mob on the platform surged and bleated.

"They're getting ready to sue," said Green.

"I'll sell them my life insurance. Reverse engine."

The train shook like a great iron dog.

"Too late, I gotta go."

"Oh God, yes. Look."

All the victims and lawyers were scrambling to pile on, and the stupid fool who had shouted "fire" was forgotten.

The train jerked with a great rumbling rattle.

"So long," whispered Green.

"Go," I said, wearily. "But who's next?"

"Next?"

"With your big damned awful Mortuary Warp. Who gets caught, gassed, and pinned?"

Green pulled out a crumpled paper.

"Some guy named Lafayette."

"Some guy? You dumb, stupid sap! Don't you know Lafayette saved our Revolution, age twenty-one, brought us guns, ships, uniforms, men!?"

"It doesn't say that here." Green stared at his notes.

"Lafayette was Washington's adopted son. Went home and named his firstborn George Washington Lafayette."

"They left that out," said Green.

"Came back, age seventy, paraded eighty cities where people named streets, parks, and towns for him. Lafayette, Lafayette, Lafayette."

"Hey!" Green poked the note. "Yeah, Lafayette's *second* farewell tour."

The train gave an assassin's cry, the wheels ground their teeth.

"See you in Springfield." Green jumped up onto the back platform. "Next April."

"Who's that with you?" I shouted.

Green turned and yelled.

"Booth," he cried. "John Wilkes Booth. He lectures from this observation car up ahead."

"Poor son of a bitch," I whispered.

Green read my lips and repeated, "Poor S.O.B."

And the train moved on.

a CAREFUL MAN DIES

1946

YOU SLEEP ONLY FOUR HOURS A NIGHT. You go to bed at eleven and get up at three and everything is clear as crystal. You begin your day then, have your coffee, read a book for an hour, listen to the faint, far, unreal talk and music of the predawn stations and perhaps go out for a walk, always being certain to have your special police permit with you. You have been picked up before for late and unusual hours and it got to be a nuisance, so you finally got yourself a special permit. Now you can walk and whistle where you wish, hands in your pockets, heels striking the pavement in a slow, easy tempo.

This has been going on since you were sixteen years old.

You're now twenty-five, and four hours a night is still enough sleep.

You have few glass objects in your house. You shave with an electric razor, because a safety razor sometimes cuts you and you cannot afford to bleed.

You are a hemophiliac. You start bleeding and you can't stop. Your father was the same way—though he served only as a frightening example. He cut his finger once, fairly deeply, and died on the way to the hospital from blood loss. There was also hemophilia on your mother's side of the family, and that was where you got it.

In your right inside coat pocket you carry, always, a small bottle of coagulant tablets. If you cut yourself you immediately swallow them. The coagulant formula spreads through your system to supply the necessary clotting material to stop the seepage of blood.

So this is how your life goes. You need only four hours of sleep and you stay away from sharp objects. Each waking day of your life is almost twice as long as the average man's, but your life expectancy is short, so it comes to an ironic balance.

It will be long hours until the morning mail. So you tap out four thousand words on a story with your typewriter. At nine o'clock when the postal box in front of your door clicks you stack the typewritten sheets, clip them together, check the carbon copy and file them under the heading NOVEL IN PROGRESS. Then, smoking a cigarette, you go for the mail.

You take the mail from the box. A check for three hundred

dollars from a national magazine, two rejections from lesser houses, and a small cardboard box tied with green string.

After shuffling over the letters you turn to the box, untie it, flip open the top, reach in, and pull out the thing that is inside it.

"Damn!"

You drop the box. A splash of quick red spreads on your fingers. Something bright has flashed in the air with a chopping movement. There was the whir of a metal spring, whining.

Blood begins to run smoothly, swiftly from your wounded hand. You stare at it for a moment, stare at the sharp object on the floor, the little bestial contraption with the razor embedded in a springed trap that clipped shut when you pulled it out, and caught you unawares!

Fumbling, trembling, you reach into your pocket, getting blood all over yourself, and pull out the bottle of tablets and gulp several down.

Then, while you are waiting for the stuff to clot, you wrap the hand in a handkerchief and, gingerly, pick up the contraption and set it on the table.

After staring at it for ten minutes you sit down and have yourself a cigarette clumsily, and your eyelids jerk and flicker and your vision melts and hardens and remelts the objects of the room, and finally you have the answer.

. . . Someone doesn't like me. . . . Someone doesn't like me at all . . .

The phone rings. You get it.

"Douglas speaking."

"Hello, Rob. This is Jerry."

"Oh, Jerry."

"How are you, Rob?"

"Pale and shaken."

"How come?"

"Somebody sent me a razor in a box."

"Stop kidding."

"Seriously. But you wouldn't want to hear."

"How's the novel, Rob?"

"I won't ever finish it if people keep sending me sharp objects. I expect to get a cut-glass Swedish vase in the next mail. Or a magician's cabinet with a large collapsible mirror."

"Your voice sounds funny," says Jerry.

"It should. As for the novel, Gerald, it is going great guns. I've just done another four thousand words. In this scene I show the great love of Anne J. Anthony for Mr. Michael M. Horn."

"You're asking for trouble, Rob."

"I have discovered that only this minute."

Jerry mutters something.

You say, "Mike wouldn't touch me, directly, Jerry. Neither would Anne. After all, Anne and I were once engaged. That was before I found out about what they were doing. The parties they were giving, the needles they were giving people, full of morphine."

"They might try to stop the book, though, somehow."

"I believe you. They already have. This box that came in the mail. Well, maybe *they* didn't do it, but one of the other people, some of the others I mention in the book, they might take a notion."

"Have you talked to Anne recently?" asks Jerry.

"Yes," you say.

"And she still prefers that kind of life?"

"It's a wild one. You see a lot of pretty pictures when you take some kinds of narcotics."

"I wouldn't believe it of her; she doesn't look that sort."

"It's your Oedipus complex, Jerry. Women never seem like females to you. They seem like bathed, flowered, sexless ivory carvings on rococo pedestals. You loved your mother too completely. Luckily I'm more ambivalent. Anne had me fooled for a while. But she was having so much fun one night and I thought she was drunk, and then first thing I knew she was kissing me and pressing a little needle into my hand and saying, 'Come on, Rob, please. You'll like it.' And the needle was as full of morphine as Anne was."

"And that was that," says Jerry on the other end of the line.

"That was that," you say. "So I've talked to the police and the State Bureau of Narcotics, but there's a fumble somewhere and they're afraid to move. Either that or they're being handsomely paid. A little of both, I suspect. There's always someone somewhere in any one system who clogs the pipe. In the police department there's always one guy who'll take a little money on the side and spoil the good name of the force. It's a fact. You can't get away from it. People are human. So am I. If I can't clean the clog in the pipe one way, I'll clean it another. This novel of mine, needless to say, will be what will do it."

"You might go down the drain with it, Rob. Do you really think your novel will shame the narcotics boys into acting?"

"That's the idea."

"Won't you be sued?"

"I've taken care of that. I'm signing a paper with my publishers absolving them of any blame, saying that all characters in this novel are fictitious. Thus, if I've lied to the publishers they are blameless. If I'm sued, the royalties from the novel will be used in my defense. And I've got plenty of evidence. Incidentally, it's a corking good novel."

"Seriously, Rob. Did someone send you a razor in a box?"

"Yes, and there lies my greatest danger. Rather thrilling. They wouldn't dare kill me outright. But if I died of my own natural carelessness and my inherited blood makeup, who would blame them? They wouldn't slit my throat. That'd be somewhat obvious. But a razor, or a nail, or the edge of the steering wheel of my car fixed and set with knife blades . . . it's all very melodramatic. How goes it with your novel, Jerry?"

"Slow. How's about lunch today?"

"Fair enough. The Brown Derby?"

"You sure ask for trouble. You know damn well Anne eats there every day with Mike!"

"Stimulates my appetite, Gerald, old man. See you."

You hang up. Your hand is okay now. You whistle as you bandage it in the bathroom. Then you give the little razor contraption a going-over. A primitive thing. The chance were hardly fifty-fifty it would even work.

You sit down and write three thousand more words, stimulated by the early morning events.

The handle of the door to your car has been filed, sharpened to a razor edge during the night. Dripping blood, you return to the house for more bandages. You gulp pills. The bleeding stops.

After you deposit the two new chapters of the book in your safety-deposit box at the bank, you drive and meet Jerry Walters at the Brown Derby. He looks as electric and small as ever, dark-jowled, his eyes popping behind his thick-lensed glasses.

"Anne's inside." He grins at you. "And Mike's with her. Why do we wanna eat here? I ask." His grin dries and he stares at you, at your hand. "You need a drink! Right this way. There's Anne at that table over there. Nod to her."

"I'm nodding."

You watch Anne, at a corner table, in a monk's cloth sport dress, interwoven with gold and silver thread, a link of Aztec jewelry in bronze units around her tan neck. Her hair is the same bronze color. Beside her, behind a cigar and a haze of smoke, is the rather tall, spare figure of Michael Horn, who looks just like what he is, gambler, narcotics specialist, sensualist par excellence, lover of women, ruler of men, wearer of diamonds and silk undershorts. You would not want to shake hands with him. That manicure looks too sharp.

You sit down to a salad. You are eating it when Anne and Mike come by the table, after their cocktail. "Hello, sharpster," you say to Mike Horn, with a little emphasis on the latter word.

Behind Horn is his bodyguard, a young twenty-two-year-old kid from Chicago named Berntz, with a carnation in his black coat lapel and his black hair greased, and his eyes sewed down by little muscles at the corners, so he looks sad.

"Hello, Rob, darling," says Anne. "How's the book?"

"Fine, fine. I've got a swell new chapter on you, Anne."

"Thank you, darling."

"When you going to leave this big heel-headed leprechaun?" you ask her, not looking at Mike.

"After I kill him," says Anne.

Mike laughs. "That's a good one. Now let's get going, baby. I'm tired of this jerk."

You upset some cutlery. Somehow a lot of dishes fall. You almost hit Mike. But Berntz and Anne and Jerry gang up on you and so you sit down, the blood banging your ears, and people pick up the cutlery and hand it to you.

"So long," says Mike.

Anne goes out the door like a pendulum on a clock and you note the time. Mike and Berntz follow.

You look at your salad. You reach for your fork. You pick at the stuff.

You take a forkful.

Jerry stares at you. "For God's sake, Rob, what's wrong?"

You don't speak. You take the fork away from your lips.

"What's wrong, Rob? Spit it out!"

You spit.

Jerry swears under his breath.

Blood.

You and Jerry come down out of the Taft building and you are now talking sign language. A wad of stuff is in your mouth. You smell of antiseptic.

"But I don't see how," said Jerry. You gesture with your hands. "Yeah, I know, the fight in the Derby. The fork gets knocked on the floor." You gesture again. Jerry supplies the explanation to the pantomime. "Mike, or Berntz, picks it up, hands it back to you, but instead slips you a fixed, sharpened fork."

You nod your head, violently, flushing.

"Or maybe it was Anne," says Jerry.

No, you shake your head. You try to explain in pantomime that if Anne knew about this she'd quit Mike cold. Jerry doesn't get it and peers at you through his thick goggles. You sweat.

A tongue is a bad place for a cut. You knew a guy once who had a cut tongue and the wound never healed, even though it stopped bleeding. And imagine with a hemophiliac!

You gesture now, forcing a smile as you climb into your car.

Jerry squints, thinks, gets it. "Oh." He laughs. "You mean to say, all you need now is a stab in the backside?"

You nod, shake hands, drive off.

Suddenly, life is not so funny anymore. Life is real. Life is stuff that comes out of your veins at the least invitation. Unconsciously, your hand goes again and again to your coat pocket where the tablets are hidden. Good old tablets.

It is about now you notice you are being followed.

You turn left at the next corner and you're thinking fast. An accident. Yourself knocked out and bleeding. Unconscious, you'll never be able to give yourself a dose of those precious little pills you keep in your pocket.

You press the gas pedal. The car thunders ahead and you look back and the other car is still following you, gaining. A tap on the head, the least cut, and you are all done.

You turn right at Wilcox, left again when you reach Melrose, but they are still with you. There is only one thing to do.

You stop the car at the curb, take the keys, climb quietly out and walk up and sit down on somebody's lawn.

As the trailing car passes, you smile and wave at them.

You think you hear curses as the car vanishes.

You walk the rest of the way home. On the way you call a garage and have them pick up your car for you.

Though you've always been alive, you've never been as alive as you are now—you'll live forever. You're smarter than all of them put together. You're watchful. They won't be able to do a thing that you can't see and circumvent one way or another. You have that much faith in yourself. You can't die. Other people die, but not you. You have complete faith in your ability to live. There'll never be a person clever enough to kill you.

You can eat flames, catch cannonballs, kiss women who have torches for lips, chuck gangsters under the chin. Being the way you are, with the kind of blood you have in your body, has made you—a gambler? A taker of chances? There must be some way to explain the morbid craving you have for danger or near danger. Well, explain it this way. You get a terrific ego lift out of coming through each experience safely. Admit it, you're a conceited, self-satisfied person with morbid ideas of self-destruction. Hidden ideas, naturally. No one admits outwardly he wants to die, but it's in there somewhere. Self-preservation and the will to die, tugging back and forth. The urge to die getting you into messes, self-preservation yanking you out again. And you hate and laugh at these people when you see them wince and twist with discomfort when you come out, whole and intact. You feel superior, godlike, immortal. They are inferior, cowardly, common. And you are a little more than irked to think that Anne prefers her narcotics to you. She finds the needle more stimulating. Damn her! And yet—you also find her stimulating—and dangerous. But you'll take a chance with her, anytime, yes, any old time. . . .

It is once again four in the morning. The typewriter is going under your fingers as the doorbell rings. You get up and go to answer in the complete before-dawn quiet.

Far away on the other side of the universe her voice says, "Hello, Rob. Anne. Just get up?"

"Right. This is the first time you've come around in days, Anne." You open the door and she comes in past you, smelling good.

"I'm tired of Mike. He makes me sick. I need a good dose of Robert Douglas. I'm really tired, Rob."

"You sound it. My sympathies."

"Rob—" A pause.

"Yeah?"

A pause. "Rob—could we get away tomorrow? I mean, today—this afternoon. Up the coast somewhere, lie in the sun and just let it burn us? I need it, Rob, badly."

"Why, I guess so. Sure. Yeah. Hell, yes!"

"I like you, Rob. I only wish you weren't writing that damned novel."

"If you cleared out of that mob I might quit," you say. "But I don't like the things they've done to you. Has Mike told you what he's doing to me?"

"Is he doing something, darling?"

"He's trying to bleed me. *Really* bleed me, I mean. You know Mike underneath, don't you, Anne. White-livered and scared. Berntz too, for that matter. I've seen their kind before, acting tough to cover up their lily guts. Mike doesn't want to kill me. He's afraid of killing. He thinks he can scare me out of this. But I'm going ahead because I don't think he'll have enough nerve to finish it. He'd rather take a chance on a narcotics rap than go up for murder. I know Mike."

"But do you know me, darling?"

"I think I do."

"Very well?"

"Well enough."

"I might kill you."

"You wouldn't dare. You like me."

"I like myself," she purrs, "too."

"You always were a strange one. I never knew, and still don't know, what makes you tick."

"Self-preservation."

You offer her a cigarette. She is very near you. You nod wonderingly. "I saw you pull the wings off a fly once."

"It was interesting."

"Did you dissect bottled kittens in school?"

"With relish."

"Do you know what dope does to you?"

"I relish that too."

"How about this?"

You are near enough so it takes only a move to bring your faces together. The lips are as good as they look. They are warm and moving and soft.

She holds you away a bit. "I relish this also," she says.

You hold her against you, again the lips meet you and you shut your eyes. . . .

"Dammit," you say, breaking away.

Her fingernail has bitten into your neck.

"I'm sorry, darling. Hurt you?" she asks.

"Everybody wants to get into the act," you say. You take out your favorite bottle and tap out a couple pills. "God, lady, what a grip. Treat me kindly from now on. I'm tender."

"I'm sorry, I forgot myself," she says.

"That's very flattering. But if *this* is what happens when I kiss you, I'd be a bloody mess if I went any further. Wait."

More bandages on your neck. Out again to kiss her.

"Easy does it, baby. We'll take in the beach and I'll give you a lecture on the evils of running with Michael Horn."

"No matter what I say, you're going ahead with the novel, Rob?"

"Mind's made up. Where were we? Oh, yeah."

Again the lips.

You park the car atop a sun-blazed cliff a little after noon. Anne runs ahead, down the timber stairs, two hundred feet down the cliff. The wind lifts her bronze hair, she looks trim in her blue bathing suit. You follow, thoughtful. You are away from everywhere. Towns are gone, the highway empty. The beach below with the sea folding in on it is wide, barren, with big slabs of granite toppled and washed by breakers. Wading birds squeal. You watch Anne go down ahead of you. What a little fool, you think of her.

You saunter arm in arm and stand letting the sun get into you. You believe everything is clean now, and good, for a while. All life is clean and fresh, even Anne's life. You want to talk, but your voice sounds funny in the salt silence, and anyway your tongue is still sore from that sharp fork.

You wade by the waterline and Anne picks something up.

"A barnacle," she says. "Remember how you used to go diving with your rubber-rimmed helmet and trident in the good old days?"

"The good old days." You think of the time past, Anne and yourself and the things that used to work out for you together. Traveling up the coast. Fishing. Diving. But even then she was a weird creature. Didn't mind killing lobsters at all. Took a relish in cleaning them.

"You used to be so foolhardy, Rob. You still are, in fact. Took chances diving for abalones when these barnacles might have cut you, badly. Sharp as razors."

"I know," you say.

She gives the barnacle a toss. It lands near your discarded shoes. As you come back up you skirt it, careful not to step on it.

"We could have been happy," she says.

"It's nice to think so, isn't it?"

"I wish you'd change your mind," she says.

"Too late," you say.

She sighs.

A wave comes in on the shore.

You are not afraid of being here with Anne. She can do nothing to you. You can handle her. You are confident of that.

No, this will be an easy, lazy day, without event. You are alert, ready for any contingency.

You lie in the sun, and it strikes through your bones and loosens you inside and you mold to the contours of the sand. Anne is beside you, and the sun gilds her tipped nose and glitters across the minute pellets of perspiration on her brow. She talks gay talk and light talk and you are fascinated with her; how she can be so beautiful and like a hunk of serpentine thrown across your path, and be so mean and small somewhere hidden inside where you can't find it?

You lie upon your stomach and the sand is warm. The sun is warm.

"You're going to burn," she says at last, laughing.

"I suppose I am," you say. You feel very clever, very immortal.

"Here, let me put some oil on your back," she said, unfolding the shiny patent leather Chinese jigsaw of her purse. She holds up a bottle of pure yellow oil. "This'll get between you and the sun," she says. "Okay?"

"Okay," you say. You are feeling very good, very superior.

She bastes you like a pig on a spit. The bottle is suspended over you and it comes down in a twine of liquid, yellow and glittering and cool to the small hollows of your spine. Her hand spreads it and massages it over your back. You lie, purring, eyes closed, watching the little blue and yellow bubbles dance across your shut eyelids as she pours on more of the liquid and laughs as she massages you.

"I feel cooler already," you say.

She continues to massage you for a minute or more and then she stops and sits beside you quietly. A long time passes and you lie deep, baked in a sand oven, not wanting to move. The sun suddenly is not so hot.

"Are you ticklish?" asks Anne, behind your back.

"No," you say, your mouth turning up at the corners.

"You have a lovely back," she says. "I'd love to tickle it."

"Tickle away," you say.

"Are you ticklish here?" she asks.

You feel a distant, sleepy movement on your back.

"No," you say.

"Here?" she says.

You feel nothing. "You aren't even touching me," you say.

"I read a book once," she says. "It said that the sensory portions of the back are so poorly developed that most people couldn't tell exactly where they were being touched."

"Nuts," you say. "Touch me. Go ahead. I'll tell you."

You feel three long movements on your back.

"Well?" she asks.

"You tickled me down under one shoulder blade for a distance of five inches. Likewise under the other shoulder blade. And then right down my spine. So there."

"Smart boy. I quit. You're too good. I need a cigarette. Damn, I'm all out. Mind if I run up to the car and get some?"

"I'll go," you say.

"Never mind." She is off across the sand. You watch her

run, lazily, sleepily, in patterns of rising hot atmosphere. You think it rather strange she is taking her purse and bottled liquid with her. Women. But all the same you cannot help but notice she is beautiful, running. She climbs up the wooden steps, turns and waves and smiles. You smile back, move your hand in a brief, lazy salute. "Hot?" she cries.

"I'm drenched," you cry back, lazily.

You feel the sweat crawling on your body. The heat is in you now and you sink down into it, as into a bath. You feel the sweat pouring down your back in torrents, faint and far away, like ants crawling on you. Sweat it out, you think. Sweat it all out. Streaks of sweat well down your ribs and along your stomach, tickling. You laugh. God, what a sweat. You never sweated like this before in your life. The smell of that oil Anne put on you is sweet in the warm air. Drowsy, drowsy.

You start. You head yanks upward.

On top of the cliff, the car is started, put in gear, and now, as you watch, Anne waving to you, the car flashes in the sun, turns, and drives away down the highway.

Just like that.

"Why you little witch!" you cry irritably. You start to get up.

You can't. The sun has made you weak. Your head swims. Damn it. You've been sweating.

Sweating.

You smell something new on the hot air. Something as familiar and timeless as the salt smell of the sea. A hot, sweet, sickish odor. An odor that is all the terror in the world to you and those of your kind. You cry out and stagger up.

You are wearing a cloak, a garment of scarlet. It clings to your thighs, and as you watch, it encases your loins and spreads and grows upon your legs and ankles. It is red. The reddest red in the color chart. The purest, loveliest, most terrible red you have ever seen, spreading and growing and pulsing along your body.

You clutch at your back. You mouth meaningless words. Your hands close upon three long open wounds cut into your flesh below the shoulder blades!

Sweat! You thought you were sweating. And it was blood! You lay there thinking it was sweat coming out of you, laughing about it, enjoying it!

You can feel nothing. Your fingers scrabble clumsily, weakly. Your back feels nothing. It is insensible.

"Here, let me put some oil on your back," says Anne, far away in the shimmering nightmare of your memory. *"You're going to burn."*

A wave crashes on the shore. In memory you see the long yellow twine of liquid pouring down on your back, suspended from Anne's lovely fingers. You feel her massaging you.

Narcotic in solution. Novocain or cocaine or something in a yellow solution that, after it clung to your back a while, deadened every nerve. Anne knows all about narcotics, doesn't she?

Sweet, sweet, lovely Anne.

"Are you ticklish?" asks Anne, in your mind again.

You retch. And echoing in your blood-red swimming mind, you give an answer: *No. Tickle away. Tickle away. Tickle away . . . Tickle away, Anne J. Anthony, lovely lady. Tickle away.*

With a nice sharp barnacle shell.

You were diving for abalones offshore and you scraped your back on a rock, in rough streaks, with a crop of razor-sharp barnacles. Yes, that's it. Diving. Accident. What a pretty setup.

Sweet, lovely Anne.

Or did you have your fingernails honed on a whetstone, my darling?

The sun bangs in your brain. The sand is beginning to melt under you. You try to find the buttons to unbutton, to rip away this red garment. Senselessly, blindly, gropingly, you search for buttons. There are none. The garment stays. How silly, you think, foolishly. *How silly to be found in your long, red woolen underwear. How silly.*

There must be zippers somewhere. Those three long cuts can be zipped up tight and then that sliding red stuff will stop sliding out of you. You, the immortal man.

The cuts aren't too deep. If you can get to a doctor. If you can take your tablets.

Tablets!

You fall forward on your coat, and search one pocket and then another pocket, and then another, and turn it inside out, and rip the lining loose and shout and cry and four waves come pounding in on the shore behind you, like trains passing, roaring. And you go back through each empty pocket again, hoping that you have missed one. But there is nothing but lint, a box of matches, and two theater ticket stubs. You drop the coat.

"Anne, come back!" you cry. "Come back! It's thirty miles to town, to a doctor. I can't walk it. I haven't time."

At the bottom of the cliff you look up. One hundred and fourteen steps. The cliff is sheer and blazing in the sun.

There is nothing to be done but climb the steps.

Thirty miles to town, you think. Well, what is thirty miles?

What a splendid day for a walk.

The Cat's Pajamas

2003

It is not every night driving along Millpass, California's Route 9, that one expects to spy a cat in the middle lane.

For that matter, it is not every evening that such a cat could be found on any untrafficked road, the cat being, more or less, an abandoned kitten.

Nevertheless, the small creature was there, busily cleaning itself, when two things happened:

A car traveling east at a rapid rate suddenly braked to a halt.

Simultaneously, a much more rapid convertible, traveling west, almost ruptured its tires to a dead standstill.

The doors of both cars banged wide in unison.

The small beast remained calm as high heels clattered one way and golfing brogans banged the other.

Almost colliding over the self-grooming creature, a handsome young man and a more than handsome young woman bent and reached.

Both hands touched the cat simultaneously.

It was a warm, round, velvet black ball with whiskers from which two great yellow eyes stared and a small pink tongue protruded.

The cat assumed a belated look of surprise as both travelers stared at the placement of their hands on its body.

"Oh no you don't!" cried the young woman.

"Oh no I don't *what?*" cried the young man.

"Let go of my cat!"

"Since when is it yours?"

"I got here first."

"It was a tie."

"Wasn't."

"Was."

He pulled at the back and she at the front and suddenly the cat *meowed*.

Both let go.

Instantly they re-seized the beautiful creature, this time the young woman grabbing the back and the young man the front.

They stared at each other for a long moment, trying to decide what to say.

"I love cats," she explained at last, not able to meet his gaze.

"So do I," he cried.

"Keep your voice down."

"Nobody can hear."

They looked both ways on the road. There was no traffic.

She blinked at the cat, as if trying to find some revelation.

"My cat died."

"So did mine," he countered.

This softened their hold on the beast.

"When?" she asked.

"Monday," he replied.

"Last Friday," she said.

They rearranged their hands on the small creature and did not so much hold as touch.

There was a moment of embarrassed silence.

"Well," he said at last.

"Yes, well," she said.

"Sorry," he said, lamely.

"The same," she said.

"What are we going to do? We can't stand here forever."

"Looks like," she said, "we're both needy."

For no reason at all he said, "I wrote an article for *Cat Fancy*."

She looked at him more intensely.

"I chaired a cat show in Kenosha," she offered.

They stood, agonizing on their new silence.

A car roared down the road past them. They jumped away

and when the car was gone saw that they both still held the wonderful creature, carrying it out of harm's way.

He stared off down the road. "There's a diner down there, I see its lights. Why don't we go have coffee and discuss the future?"

"There's no future without my cat," she said.

"Or mine, either. Come on. Follow me."

He removed the kitten from her hands.

She cried and reached out.

"It's okay," he said. "Follow me."

She backed off, got into her car, and followed him down the road.

THEY WALKED INTO THE EMPTY DINER, sat in a booth, and placed the kitten on the table between them.

The waitress glanced at them and the cat, walked off, and returned with a full saucer of cream, placing it on the table with a vast smile. They realized they were in the presence of another cat person.

The cat began to lap at the cream as the waitress brought coffee.

"Well, here we are," the young man said. "How long is this going to last? Are we going to talk all night?"

The waitress was still standing before them.

"I'm afraid it's closing time," she said.

On impulse, the young man said, "Look at us."

The waitress looked.

"If you were going to give this kitten to one of us," he said, "which one would it be?"

The waitress studied the young woman and the young man and said, "Thank God I'm not King Solomon." She wrote up the check and put it down. "There are people, you see, who still read the Bible."

"Is there another place we can go to talk?" said the young man.

The waitress nodded out the window. "There's a hotel down the road. They don't mind pets."

That caused both young people to half-jump from their seats.

Ten minutes later they walked into the hotel.

Glancing over, they saw that the bar was already dark.

"This is stupid," she said, "to let myself be brought here for the ownership of my cat."

"Not yours yet," he said.

"It won't be long," she said and glanced at the front desk.

"It's okay." He held the cat up. "This kitten will protect you. It will stand between you and me."

He carried the kitten to the front desk, where the man in charge took one look and placed a key on the signature book and handed them a pen.

Five minutes later they watched the kitten run happily into the suite's bathroom.

"Have you ever," he mused, "when you got on an elevator,

refused to discuss the weather, but told a story about your favorite cat? By the top floor, there's a wild mixture of sounds from your fellow travelers."

At which point the kitten ran back into the room.

The kitten jumped on the bed and settled itself in the middle of a pillow in the center of the bed. Seeing this, the young man commented, "Just what I was going to suggest. If we need to rest while we talk we just let the cat keep to the middle of the bed and we can lie, fully dressed, on each side to discuss our problem. Whichever of us the cat moves to first and chooses as future owner, that one gets the cat. Okay?"

"You've got some trick up your sleeve," she said.

"No," he said. "Whichever way the cat goes, that person becomes the owner."

The cat on its pillow was almost asleep.

The young man tried to think of something to say because the vast bed lay unoccupied, save by the slumbering beast. It suddenly popped into his head to speak across the bed to the young woman.

"What's your name?" he said.

"What?"

"Well," he said, "if we're going to argue till dawn about my cat—"

"Till dawn, nonsense! Midnight, maybe. *My* cat, you mean. Catherine."

"Beg pardon?"

"Silly, but my name's Catherine."

"Don't tell me your nickname." He almost laughed.

"I won't. Yours?"

"You won't believe it. Tom." He shook his head.

"I've known a dozen cats with that name."

"I don't live by it."

He tested the bed as if it were a warm bath, waiting.

"You can stand if you wish, but as for me—"

He arranged himself on the bed.

The kitten snoozed on.

With his eyes shut he said, "Well?"

She sat, and then lay on the far side, prepared to fall.

"That's more like it. Where were we?"

"Proving which of us deserves to go home with Electra."

"You've named the cat?"

"A noncommittal name, based on personality, not on sex."

"You didn't look then?"

"Nor shall I. Electra. Proceed."

"My plea for ownership? Well." He rummaged the space behind his eyelids.

He lay looking at the ceiling for a moment and then said, "You know, it's funny the way things work out with cats. When I was a kid my grandparents told me and my brothers to drown a litter of kittens. We kids went out and they did it, but I couldn't stand it and ran away."

There was a long silence.

She looked at the ceiling and said, "Thank God for that."

There was another silence and then he said, "An even more peculiar but better thing happened a few years ago. I went to a pet shop in Santa Monica, looking for a cat. They must've had twenty or thirty cats there, all kinds. I was looking around and the saleslady pointed to one cat and said, 'This one really needs help.'

"I looked at the cat, and it looked like it had been put in a washing machine and tumbled. I said, 'What happened?' She said, 'This cat belonged to someone who beat it, so it's scared of everyone.'

"I looked into the cat's eyes and then I said, 'This is the one I'll take home.'

"So I gathered the cat up and he was terrified and I took him home, put him down in the house, and he ran downstairs and wouldn't come out of the basement.

"It took me more than a month of going down to the basement and leaving food and cream until finally I lured him out, step by step. And then he became my pal.

"That's quite a difference in stories, isn't it?"

"Gosh," she said. "Yeah."

The room was dark now and very quiet. The little kitten lay on the pillow between them, and both looked over to see how the cat was doing.

It was sound asleep.

They lay, studying the ceiling.

"I've got something to tell you," she said after a while, "that I've put off saying, because it sounds like a special plea."

"Special plea?" he said.

"Well," she said, "at home, at this very moment, I have a piece of material I've cut and sewn into something for my little cat who died a week ago."

"What kind of material is that?" he said.

"Well," she said, "it's a pair of cat's pajamas."

"Oh my God!" He exhaled. "You've won. This small beast here is yours."

"Oh no!" she cried. "That's not fair."

"Anyone," he said, "who makes a pair of pajamas to fit a cat deserves to be the winner of the contest. This guy is yours."

"I can't do that," she said.

"It's my pleasure," he said.

They lay for a long while in silence. Finally she said, "You know, you're not half so bad."

"Half so bad as what?"

"As what I thought when I first met you."

"What's that sound?" he asked.

"I think I'm crying," she said.

"Let's sleep for a while," he said at last.

The moon went down the ceiling.

THE SUN ROSE.

He lay on his side of the bed, smiling.

She lay on her side of the bed, smiling.

The small kitten lay on the pillow between them.

At last, watching the sunlight in the window, she said, "Did the cat move either way during the night to indicate which of us it was going to belong to?"

"No," he said, smiling. "The cat didn't move. But *you* did."

TRIaNGLe

1951

SHE TRIED THREE DRESSES, and none fit her body. They belonged, in that moment, to someone else. Excitement changed her color so it went with none of her clothes. The glow so expanded her slender flesh that everything seemed corseted. Then the powder spilled to the floor like snow and she painted her lips upside down and blinked in the mirror as if she had seen a ghost.

"My land, Lydia." Helen stood in the doorway. "He's only a man."

"He's John Larsen," said Lydia.

"That's even worse. His hair doesn't fit his head, his arms

are too long, his mouth is thin, his eyes are like a squirrel's, and he's only up to *here*."

Lydia was crying. She sat watching the tears in the mirror.

"I'm sorry," said Helen. "But he's such a fool."

"Helen!"

"You're my own baby sister, that's all."

"I think he's God."

"Don't cry anymore. Anyone you say is God is God. It's just with our folks dead, I'm mother now, I want things right for you. I've had enough men experiences to know they are foolish liars, the whole bunch. Right out of the carnival—apes, clowns and calliope tooters."

Lydia was in a summer dream. "I think he's kind, handsome, and good. He tips his hat on the street to us. He's never come to our house before, has he? Never said boo. And then, suddenly, calling me on the phone today, saying he'd like to drop by for an hour to see me. I cried all afternoon, I was so happy. I've wanted him to call for years. I've seen him in front of the United Cigar store ever since I was sixteen years old, that was twenty years ago, and always wanted to stop and say, I love you, John, take me away from all this, be mine. But I always kept walking. And, do you know, once in a while, in recent years, when you and I walked by, it seemed there was something in his eyes, as if he were noticing me too. But he always smiled and tipped his hat."

"Men teach each other tricks like that. A front like a palace, and all outhouse and stucco behind. Put your face back on and wear something green to go with your red complexion."

"I didn't mean to cry it red." She looked at the old mouth on her wadded kerchief. "Helen, Helen, was it like this for you, ten years back, when you loved Jamie Josephs?"

"My bedclothes were cinders every morning."

"Oh, Helen!"

"But then I found he was playing that shell game you see at circuses. He asked me to bet everything on a hunch. I was young. I did. I bet that if I spent of myself freely, when the time came I'd know where to find him. But the time came and I lifted up one of three shells and Jamie wasn't there. He'd moved his little act up the street, and out of town on the Skokie Limited. I wonder if *any* woman ever found Jamie?"

"Oh, don't, let's be happy tonight!"

"You be happy by being happy. I'll be happy by being cynical, and we'll *see* who's happiest in the long run."

Lydia painted a new mouth and made it smile.

It was a tender evening in September, the first smoky fire starting in the maples around the old, softening house. Lydia floated in the cavernous living room, lights out, only her face a pink lamp, so she could see him far away, like a figure in a melodrama, before he turned and rustled the leaves crisply on the front sidewalk. She heard him whistling an autumn song, down the street. She hurried over her speeches, and suddenly the words were a crumpled series of started but unfinished letters to her own spirit and flesh, heaped and blown about her mind. She started to cry again, and this made the precious words run and blur, the polite stage instructions to her hands and feet threatened to be lost forever. She stopped the process by slapping herself, once, on the side of her face. Now he was walking up the steps to the silent house, now he sounded the silver doorbell, taking off his straw hat, which was a trifle late for the season, and clearing his throat three times, a customer demanding service from an inattentive clerk. He muttered under his breath, as if he too were shuffling the lines of his part, abysmally.

"Good evening!"

As if a gun had gone off in his face, John Larsen fell back from the door. Staggered by the sound of her own voice suddenly exploded from her mouth, Lydia could only sway in the doorway until the man out there found his smile and used it. Then, somehow, she opened the door and stepped out onto the porch.

"It's such a nice night," she said. "Let's sit in the porch swing."

"Fine," said John Larsen, and they sat in the shadowy vined, secret porch swing, away from the gaze of the town. He helped her elbow into the swing, and where he had touched was a brand that smoked and ached and promised to leave a scar for the rest of her life. She sat down dizzily, and the world moved this way, that way, she thought herself sick and then discovered it was the swing taking her up and down and this man still silent, wretchedly turning his hat in his hands, reading the size tag with his small eyes, reading the label and the old price-insertion. The hat sounded like a piece of wicker furniture in his lap. He kept reaching into it to find his first speech and then, in confusion, looked as if he might get up and bolt the evening. Somewhere between the sidewalk and here he had lost his notes.

Out of a face that was a roaring torch, the flesh sunburned by her blood, the bones aching with warmth, Lydia felt her puffed mouth say, "It's nice to see you, Mr. Larsen."

"Oh, call me John," he replied, and propelled the swing with his shoes that now, with demon voices, squeaked at every motion.

"We've been hoping that someday you might drop by," said Lydia, and then realized it was too much to say.

"Have you, have you really?" He turned and gazed at her with childish delight, so it was all right, what she had said.

"Yes, we've often said we'd like you to drop by."

"I'm glad," he said, on the edge of the swing. "You know, it's a very important thing I've come to talk about tonight."

"I realize."

"Do you? Have you guessed?"

"I think I have."

"I've known you sisters for a good many years, to speak to in passing," he said. "I've seen you walking by together so many times. And I never got up the courage—"

"To ask to come to the house."

"That's right. Until tonight. And then today I got the

courage. Do you know why? Today's my thirty-fourth birthday. And I said to myself, John Larsen, you're getting old. You've been a drummer too long, you've traveled too much. The gay life's dead for you. Time to settle down. And what better place to settle than Green Town, your own hometown, and there's a certain girl there, really beautiful, maybe she's never looked at you—"

"But she has—" said Lydia, obliquely.

He looked stunned and happy. "I never dreamt!"

He leaned back in the swing, grinning. "Anyway, I said to myself, you ought to go call. Make yourself known. Spit it out. I never dared. You see, women can be so beautiful and far away, untouchable, the right kind of women. And I'm a coward. I really am, about women. The correct women. So what do you suggest I do? I had to come and see you first, to talk to you, to plan things, to see if you could help me."

"First?" said Lydia. "Help you? Plan things."

"Oh, your sister's really lovely," said John Larsen. "Tall and pale. I think of her like a white lily. The long-stemmed variety. So stately and grave and beautiful. I've watched her passing by for years and been in love with her, there I've said it, for ten years I've seen her walk by but I was afraid to say anything."

"What?" The torch flickered in her face and went out.

"So you say she likes me too? To think all these years wasted. I should have come sooner. Will you help me? Will you tell her, will you break the ice? Will you arrange for me to come see her soon?"

"You're in love with my sister." It was a statement of fact.

"With all my heart."

She felt like a stove on a winter's morning, when all the ashes are dead and all the wood is cold and frosted over.

"What's the matter?" he asked.

She sat and the world rocked and this time she was really ill. The world dipped.

"Say something," he pleaded.

"You love my sister," she said.

"The way you say that."

"I love you," she said.

"What?"

"I love you," she said.

"Now wait a minute," he said.

"Didn't you hear me?" she asked.

"I don't understand."

"I don't either," she said, sitting straight. Now the trembling stopped and the coldness was coming out her eyes.

"You're crying," he said.

"It's so silly," she said. "You think about me the same way *she* thinks about you."

"Oh, no," he protested.

"Oh, yes," she said, not touching the tears with her hands.

"That can't be," he almost yelled.

"It is."

"But *I* love her," he said.

"But *I* love you," she replied.

"Don't you think there's a little spark of love in her for me?" he wanted to know, reaching out in the air of the porch.

"Don't you think you could have a little spark of love in yourself for me?" she said.

"There must be something I can do."

"There's nothing any of us can do. Everybody loves the wrong one, everybody hates the wrong one." She began to laugh.

"Don't laugh."

"I'm not laughing." She threw her head back.

"Stop that!"

"I will." She yelled out her laughter, and her eyes were wet and he was shaking her.

"Stop that!" he yelled into her face, standing up now. "Go in and tell your sister to come out, tell her I want to see her!"

"Tell her yourself, go tell her yourself."

The laughing went on.

He put his hat on and stood there, bewildered, looking at her swinging hysterically in the swing, like a hunk of cold iron, and looking at the house. "Cut it out!" he cried.

He was starting to shake Lydia again when a voice said, "Stop that!"

He turned and there was Helen, behind the front porch screen, in cool shadow, only a paleness, a dim chalk outline.

"Get away from her, leave her alone. Take your hands off her, Mister Larsen."

"But, Helen!" he protested, running to the screen. The door was hooked and she put her hand out, as if tapping the screen to loose from it the last flies of the old summer.

"Get off the porch, please," said Helen.

"Helen, let me in!"

John, come back! thought Lydia.

"I'll give you until I count to ten to get your hat and run."

He stood between the two cold ladies on the dark porch. Summer and autumn both were gone now. An invisible snow fell upon his shoulders and a wind came up from the interior of the house.

"How did this all happen?" He turned in a circle to the world, slowly. Somehow, to Helen, he seemed like a man on a shore and a boat, carrying her, the house that is, drawing out into the autumnal sea and nobody waving good-bye, but everyone separating forever. She could not quite decide whether he was handsome or ridiculous. The great horn of the sea was blowing and the ship moved away faster, leaving him stranded on the lawn, picking up his hat, looking into it, as if to see his entire life ahcad of him, and the size of it was very small and the price tag was low indeed. His hands shook. He was drunk with shock. He reeled. His eyes wobbled in his pale face.

"Good night, Mister Larsen," said Helen, hid in the dark.

Lydia was swinging in the swing, silent, breathless now.

Not laughing or crying, just letting the dark world ride in stars one way, and the white moon another, just a body in a whirling arc, her hands at her sides, the tears drying on her face in the wind that she stirred by sailing.

"Good-bye." Mr. Larsen stumbled and fell, half across the lawn. He sat there a moment, as if he were drowning, putting his hands up in the air. Then he got up and ran away down the street.

After he was gone, Helen opened the door and came slowly out to sit in the swing.

They rocked for about ten minutes that way, silently. Then Helen said, "I don't suppose there's any way you can stop loving him?"

They swung in the night.

"No."

A minute later Lydia said, "I don't suppose there's any way for *you* to find a way to love him, is there?"

Helen shook her head.

The next idea to come to them was shared. One started and the other finished it.

"I don't suppose there's any way—"

"—he could stop loving you, Helen."

"—and love you instead, Lydia?"

They gave the swing a push in the grape-arbor night, and after the fourth swing back and forth, they said, "No."

"I can see us," said Helen. "Good God. Twenty, thirty years from now. You and me out walking for an evening downtown. Us walking along Main Street, talking, alone. And coming to the cigar store. And there he is. There's John Larsen, all by himself, under the cigar store light, unwrapping a cigar. And we sort of slow down and he stops lighting the cigar when he sees us. And I look at him the way I look at him now. And you look at him the way you look at him now. And he looks at you the only way he can look at you. And at me the fool's way he looked at me tonight. And then we sort of stand there and you and I nod. And he puts up his hand and tips his hat. And he's bald. And we're both gray. And we walk on. Arm in arm. And do our shopping and spend the evening around town. And when we come back, two hours later, on our way home, he's still standing there, alone, looking off into nothing."

They let the cat die.

They sat there, not moving, thinking of the next thirty years.

THE MAFIOSO CEMENT-MIXING MACHINE

2003

BURNHAM WOOD, I never knew his real name, led me into his splendid garage, which he had converted into a workplace/library.

On the shelves stood the complete works of F. Scott Fitzgerald, bound in rich leather, with gold epaulettes.

My hands itched as I studied this incredible collection, part of a literary experiment he was planning.

Burnham Wood turned from his amazing library, winked, and pointed at the far end of his vast garage.

"There!" he said. "My ironic machine with a peculiar name. What?"

With no particular emotion I said, "It looks like one of

those trucks that revolve on their axis every ten seconds, churning cement slag on its way to pouring new roads."

"Touché!" said Burnham Wood. "It's my Mafioso Cement Mixer. Look around. There's a relationship between it and this library."

I glanced at the books but found no relationship. Burnham Wood patted the side of his machine, which stood, rumbling, like a great gray elephant. The Mafioso Machine shivered and stopped.

"The idea struck," said Burnham Wood, "one desert night when a cement mixer passed me at high speed. I wondered if it was on its way to make concrete boots for lost Italian gangsters. I laughed, but the idea haunted me and woke me in the middle of the night months later. I had to fuse my library with this great monster, find a way, I thought, to travel this cement elephant back in time."

I skirted the great gray beast as it tumbled and whispered, rotating and ready to travel.

"The Mafioso Cement-Mixing Machine?" I said. "Explain."

Burnham Wood touched the F. Scott Fitzgerald books on their shelf and placed one in my hands.

I opened the book. "*The Last Tycoon,* by F. Scott Fitzgerald. His last. He didn't live to finish it."

"Here then." Burnham Wood stroked his great machine. "Shall I tell you what's inside? All the seconds, minutes, hours, days, weeks, months, and years of time, going back fifty years. We're going to run those hours and days to help

Scotty get some extra time to finish this novel. It was going to be his best but wound up a half-broken record played late nights while we drank far too much."

"And," I said, "just how are you going to do this?"

Burnham Wood produced a list. "Read. Those are the destinations my machine will visit to do the job."

I stared at the list and began to read.

"B. P. Schulberg, Paramount, right?"

"Right."

"Irving Thalberg, MGM? Darryl Zanuck, Fox?"

"Correct."

"Will you visit all these people?"

"Yes."

"You have directors at various studios, producers, floozies he once knew, bartenders all over creation. What will you do with them?"

"Find ways to move them, bribe them, or, when necessary, beat them up."

"What about Irving Thalberg? He died in 1936, right?"

"And if he'd lived a bit longer he might have been a good influence on Scotty."

"What are you going to do about a dead man?"

"When Thalberg died there was no sulfanilamide in the world. I'd like to sneak into his hospital room the week before his death and give him the medicines that might cure him and let him go back to MGM for another year. He might have hired Scotty for something better than the things they gave him."

"That's quite a list," I said. "You sound like you're going to move these people like chess pieces."

Burnham Wood showed me a flush of hundred-dollar bills. "I'm going to spread these around. Some of these moguls might be tempted to move. Stand close. Listen."

I stood close to the great rumbling machine. From its interior I heard far cries and gunshots.

"It sounds like a revolution," I said.

"Bastille," said Burnham Wood.

"Why would that be inside?"

"*Marie Antoinette,* MGM—Fitzgerald worked on it."

"My God, yes. Why would he write a thing like that?"

"He loved film, but he loved money even more. Listen again."

This time the gunfire was louder, and when the bombardment ceased I said, "*Three Comrades,* Germany, MGM, 1936."

Burnham Wood nodded.

There was a ripple of many women laughing. When it quieted I said, "*The Women,* Norma Shearer, Rosalind Russell, MGM, 1939."

Burnham Wood nodded again.

There were more cries of laughter, bursts of music. I recited the names I remembered from old film books.

"*Possessed,* Joan Crawford. *Madame Curie,* Greer Garson, screenplay by Huxley and F. Scott Fitzgerald. My God," I said. "Why did he bother with all that and why are all those sounds inside your machine?"

"I'm tearing them up, I'm destroying the scripts. It's all packed inside with the mix. *A Diamond as Big as the Ritz*, *This Side of Paradise*, *Tender Is the Night*. All of them are in there. When you mix all that junk with the really good stuff you've got a chance of laying out a new road somewhere in the past to make a new future."

I reread the list. "Those are the names of producers and directors and fellow writers over a period of years; some at MGM, a few at Paramount, and more in New York City as late as the summer of 1939. What's the sum?"

I glanced up at Burnham Wood and saw that he was trembling with anticipation, glancing at the machine.

"I'm going to run back with my metaphorical cement mixer and pour shoes for all those idiot people and transport them to some sea of eternity and drop them in. I'll clear the way for Scotty, give him a gift of Time so that, please God, finally *The Last Tycoon* will be finished, done, and published."

"No one can do that!"

"I will, or die trying. I'm going to pick them up, one by one, on special days in all those years. I'm going to kidnap them out of their environments and deliver them to other towns in other years, where they'll have to make their way, blindly, having forgotten where they came from and the stupid burden they laid on Scotty."

I brooded, eyes shut. "Good Lord, this reminds me of a George Arliss film I saw when I was a kid. *The Man Who Played God*."

Burnham Wood laughed quietly. "George Arliss, yes. I do feel somewhat like the Creator. I dare to be the Savior of our dear, drunken, foolish, childish Fitzgerald."

He stroked the machine again, and it trembled and whispered. I could almost hear the siren of the years rushing and tumbling inside.

"It's time," said Burnham Wood. "I'm going to climb in, turn the rheostats, and do a disappearing act. An hour from now, go to the nearest bookstore or check the books on my shelf and see if there's any change. I don't know if I'll ever return, I may get locked in some year a long while back. I may get as lost as the people I plan to kidnap."

"I hope you don't mind my saying," I said, "but I don't think you can mess with time, no matter how dearly you might wish to be the coeditor of F. Scott Fitzgerald's last book."

Burnham Wood shook his head. "I lie in bed many nights and worry over the deaths of many of my favorite authors. Poor sad Melville, dear lost Poe, Hemingway, who should have been killed in that African plane crash, but it only killed his ability to be a fine writer. I can do nothing about those, but here, in striking distance of Hollywood, I must try. That's it." Burnham Wood brisked his hands and reached out and shook mine. "Wish me luck."

"Luck," I said. "Is there anything I can say to stop you?"

"Don't," he said. "My great American elephant beast here will tumble time inside its guts, not cement, but the hours, days, and years—a literary device."

He climbed into his Mafioso Cement-Mixing Machine, did some adjustments on a computerized bank, then turned to study me.

"What will you do an hour from now?" he asked.

"Buy a new copy of *The Last Tycoon*," I said.

"Great!" cried Burnham Wood. "Stand back. Beware the concussion!"

"That's from *Shape of Things to Come*, yes?"

"H. G. Wells." Burnham Wood laughed. "Beware the concussion!"

The lid clanged shut. The great Mafioso Cement-Mixing Machine rumbled, turned in the years, and the garage was suddenly empty.

I waited a long while, hoping that another concussion might cause the great gray beast to suddenly reappear, but the garage remained empty.

At the bookstore, an hour later, I asked for a particular book.

The salesman handed me a copy of *The Last Tycoon.*

I opened it and turned the pages.

A loud cry came from my gaping mouth.

"He did it!" I shouted. "He did it! There are fifty more pages and the end is not the end that I read when the book was published many years ago. He did it, by God, he did it!"

Tears sprang from my eyes.

"That will be twenty-four dollars and fifty cents," said the salesman. "What gives?"

"You'll never know," I said. "But *I* know and all blessings to Burnham Wood."

"Who's he?"

"The man who played God," I replied.

Fresh tears burned my eyes, and I pressed the book to my heart and walked from the store muttering, "Oh yes, the man who played God."

THE GHOSTS

1950–1952

AT NIGHT THE GHOSTS floated like milkweed pod in the white meadows. Far off you could see their lantern eyes aglow, and a fitful flaring of fire when they knocked together, as if someone had shaken a brazier down and live coals were cascading from the jolt in a little fiery shower. They came under our windows, I remember well, every midsummer night for three weeks each year. And each year Papa would seal up our south windows and herd us children like small puppies into another room around north where we would spend our nights hoping the ghosts would change their direction and entertain us on our new meadow slope below. But no. The south meadow was theirs.

"They must be from Mabsbury," said Father, his voice drifting up the hall stairs to where we three lay in bed. "But when I run out with my gun, by George, they're gone!"

We heard Mother's voice reply, "Well, put your gun away. You wouldn't shoot them anyhow."

It was Father who told us girls that the ghosts *were* ghosts. He nodded gravely and looked us in the eye. The ghosts were *indecent,* he said. For they laughed and pressed their shapes into the meadow grass. You could see where they had lain the night before, one a man, one a woman. Always laughing softly. We children woke and bent out our windows to let the wind flutter our dandelion hair, listening.

Each year we tried to shield the coming of the ghosts from Mother and Father. Sometimes we succeeded for as much as a week. Along about July 8, however, Father would begin to get nervous. He would pry at us and handle us and peer through our curtains as he asked, "Laura, Ann, Henrietta—have you—that is, at night—in the last week or so—have you *noticed* anything?"

"Anything, Papa?"

"Ghosts, I mean."

"*Ghosts,* Papa?"

"You know, like last summer and the summer before."

"I haven't seen anything, have you, Henrietta?"

"I haven't, have you, Ann?"

"No, have you, Laura?"

"Stop it, *stop* it!" cried Father. "Answer a simple question. Have you heard anything?"

"I heard a rabbit."

"I saw a dog."

"There was a cat—"

"Well, you must tell me if the ghosts return," he said, earnestly, and edged away, blushing.

"Why doesn't he want us to see the ghosts?" whispered Henrietta. "After all, Papa's the one who said they *were* ghosts."

"I *like* ghosts," said Ann. "They're *different*."

That was true. For three small girls, ghosts were rare and wonderful. Our tutors drove to see us every day and kept us strictly laced. There were birthday parties, now and then, but mostly our lives were plain as pound cake. We longed for adventure. The ghosts saved us, supplying us with enough goose pimples to last the season through and over until next year.

"What brings the ghosts here?" wondered Ann.

We did not know.

Father seemed to know. We heard his voice floating up the stairwell again one night. "The quality of the moss," he said to Mama.

"You make too much of it," she said.

"I think they've come back."

"The girls haven't said."

"The girls are a bit too sly. I think we'd better change their room tonight."

"Oh dear." Mama sighed. "Let's wait until we're sure. You know how the girls are when they change rooms. They don't sleep well for a week and are grumpy all day. Think of *me*, Edward."

"All right," said Father, but his voice was clever and planning.

The next morning we three girls raced down to breakfast, playing tag. "You're it!" we cried, and stopped and stared at Papa. "Papa, what's wrong?"

For there was Papa, his hands thick with yellow ointments and white bandages. His neck and face looked red and irritated.

"Nothing," he said, gazing deep into his cereal, stirring it darkly.

"But what happened?" We gathered about him.

"Come away, children," said Mother, trying not to smile. "Father has poison ivy."

"Poison ivy?"

"How did *that* happen, Papa?"

"Sit down, children," warned Mother, for Father was quietly grinding his teeth.

"How *did* he get poisoned?" I asked.

Papa stamped from the room. We said nothing else.

THE NEXT NIGHT, the ghosts were gone.

"Oh, heck," said Ann.

In our beds, like mice, we waited for midnight.

"Hear anything?" I whispered. I saw Henrietta's doll eyes at the window, looking down.

"No," she said.

"What time is it?" I hissed, later.

"Two o'clock."

"I guess they're not coming," I said, sadly.

"Guess they're not," said my sisters.

We listened to our small breathing in the room. The night was silent all through until dawn.

"TEA FOR TWO and two for tea," sang Father, pouring his breakfast drink. He chuckled and patted himself on the back. "Ha ha ha," he said.

"Papa's happy," said Ann to Mama.

"Yes, dear."

"Even in spite of his poison ivy."

"In spite of it," Papa said, laughing. "I'm a magician. An exorcist!"

"A *what,* Papa?"

"E-x-o-r-c-i-s-t." He spelled. "Tea, Mama?"

Henrietta and I ran to our library while Ann was out playing. *"Ex-or-cist,"* I read. "Here it *is*!" I underlined it. " 'One who exorcises ghosts.' "

"Run them around the block?" wondered Henrietta.

"No. Ex*or*cise, silly. 'To eliminate, to do away with.' "

"Kill?" wailed Henrietta.

We both stared, shocked, at the book.

"Has Papa killed our ghosts?" asked Henrietta, eyes filling with tears.

"He wouldn't be *that* mean."

We sat, stunned, for half an hour, getting cold and empty. At last Ann walked into the house, scratching her arms. "I found where Papa got poison ivy," she announced. "Anyone want to hear?"

"Where?" we asked, at last.

"On the slope under our window," said Ann. "All kinds of poison ivy there that was never there before!"

I closed the book, slowly. "Let's go see."

We stood on the slope, and there was the poison ivy, all loose and not rooted. Someone had found it in the forest and carried huge baskets of it here to the slope to spread about.

"Oh," gasped Henrietta.

We all thought of Father's swollen face and hands.

"The ghosts," I murmured. "Can *poison ivy* exorcise ghosts?"

"Look what it did to Papa."

We all nodded.

"Shh," I said, finger to my mouth. "Everyone get gloves. After dark, we'll carry it all away. We'll exorcise the exorcise."

"Hurray!" said everyone.

THE LIGHTS WERE OUT and the summer night was calm and sweet with flower scent. We waited in our beds, eyes gleaming like foxes in a cave.

"Nine o'clock," whispered Ann.

"Nine-thirty," she said, later.

"I hope they come," said Henrietta. "After all our work."

"Shh, listen!"

We sat up.

There in the moonlit meadows below came a whispering and a rustling as of a midsummer wind stirring all the grasses and the stars of the sky. There was a crackling sound and a gentle laughter, and as we ran on soft padding feet to our windows, to gather and freeze ourselves in expectant horror, there was a shower of demonic sparks on the grassy slope, and two misty forms moved through the shielding cover of bushes.

"Oh," we cried, and hugged one another, trembling. "They came back, they came *back*!"

"If Father knew!"

"But he doesn't. Shh!"

The night murmured and laughed and the grasses blew. We stood for a long while, and then Ann said, "I'm going down."

"What?"

"I want to know." Ann pulled away from us.

"But they might kill you!"

"I'm going."

"But ghosts, Ann!"

We heard her feet whisking down the stairs, the quiet opening of the front door. We pressed to the window screen. Ann, in her nightgown, like a velvety moth, fluttered across the yard. "God, take care of her," I prayed. For there she was, sneaking in darkness near the ghosts.

"Ah!" Ann screamed.

There were several more screams. Henrietta and I gasped. Ann raced across the yard but didn't slam the door. The ghosts blew off, as in a wind, over the hill, gone in an instant.

"*Now* look what you did!" cried Henrietta when Ann entered our room.

"Don't talk to me!" snapped Ann. "Oh, it's awful!" She marched to the window, started to yank it down. I stopped her.

"What's wrong?" I said.

"The ghosts," she sobbed, half angry, half sad. "They're gone forever. Daddy scared them away. Now, tonight, you know what was down there? You *know*?"

"What?"

"Two *people,*" shouted Ann, tears rolling down her cheeks. "A nasty man and woman!"

"Oh," we wailed.

"No more ghosts ever again," said Ann. "Oh, I *hate* Papa!"

And the rest of that summer, on moonlit evenings when the wind was right and white forms moved in the half-light in the meadow, we three girls did just what we did that last evening. We got up from our beds and walked quietly across the room and slammed the window so we couldn't hear those nasty people, and went back to bed and shut our eyes and dreamed of the days when the ghosts had drifted over, in those happy times before Daddy ruined everything.

WHERE'S MY HAT, WHAT'S MY HURRY?

2003

"TELL ME, Alma, when were we last in Paris?" he said.

"My God, Carl," Alma said, "don't you remember? Only two years ago."

"Ah yes," Carl said and wrote on his notepad. "2002." He glanced up. "And before that, Alma?"

"In 2001 of course."

"Yes, yes. 2001. And then there was 2000."

"How could you forget the new century?"

"The false new century."

"People couldn't wait. They had to celebrate a year too soon."

"Good old too soon, good old Paris. In 2000." He scribbled.

She glanced over and leaned forward. "What *are* you doing?"

"Remembering, recalling Paris. How many visits."

"How nice." She leaned back, smiling.

"Not necessarily. Were we there in 1999? I seem to recall—"

"Jane's wedding. Sam's graduation. We missed that year."

"Paris missed, 1999. There." He struck a line through the date.

"We were there in 1998, 1997, 1996."

She nodded three times.

He went down the years, all the way back to 1983.

She kept nodding.

He wrote the dates and then spent a long time looking at them.

He made some adjustments and scribbled some comments beside some of the dates and then sat for a moment, brooding.

At last he picked up the phone and punched in a number. When he reached it he said, "Aragon Travel? I want two tickets, one in my name and one with no name, today on the United flight at five to Paris. I'd appreciate your getting back to me as soon as possible."

He gave his name and credit card number.

He put down the phone.

"Paris?" said his wife. "You didn't warn me. There's no time."

"I just made up my mind a few minutes ago."

"Just like that? Still—"

"Didn't you hear? One ticket with my name. One with no name. Name to be supplied."

"But—"

"You're not going."

"But you've ordered two tickets . . ."

"Name and volunteer to be supplied."

"Volunteer?"

"I'm calling several."

"But if you only waited twenty-four hours—"

"I can't wait. I've waited twenty years."

"Twenty?!"

He jabbed the phone buttons. Far off, the phone rang, a high voice fluted.

"Estelle?" he said. "Carl. I know this is impromptu, silly, but do you have an up-to-date passport? You do. Well—" He laughed. "How would you like to fly to Paris this afternoon, five o'clock?" He listened. "No joke, serious, Paris, ten nights. Same room. Same bed. Me and you. Ten nights, all expenses paid." He listened and nodded, eyes shut. "Yes. Yeah. Yes, I see. Well yes, go on. I understand. I could only try. Maybe next time. Hey, I understand. I can take no very well. Sure. So long."

He hung up and stared at the phone.

"That was Estelle."

"I heard."

"She can't make it. Nothing personal."

"That's not how it sounded."

"Hold on."

"I'm holding."

He dialed. Another, higher voice answered.

"Angela? Carl. This is crazy, but could you meet me at United Airlines, five this afternoon, small carry-on, destination Paris, ten nights, champagne and pillow talk. Bed and breakfast. You. Me?"

The voice shrieked on the phone.

"I take it that's a yes. Wonderful!"

He hung up and could hardly stop laughing.

"That was Angela," he cried, beaming.

"So I gathered."

"No arguments."

"A happy camper. Now would you—"

"Hold on." He left the room and came back a few minutes later carrying a very small suitcase and tucking his wallet and passport inside his coat pocket.

He stood, swaying and laughing in front of his wife.

"Now," she said. "Explanations?"

"Yes."

He handed her the list he had written ten minutes ago.

"1980 through 2002," he said. "Our time in Paris, correct?"

She glanced at the list. "Correct. And?"

"We were in France together all those times?"

"Always together, yes." She scanned the list again. "But I don't see—"

"You never did. Tell me, do you recall in all our trips to Paris, how often did we make love?"

"What a strange question."

"Not strange at all. How many?"

She studied the list as if the total was there.

"You can't expect me to name the exact times."

"No," he said, "because you can't."

"Can't—?"

"Not even if you tried."

"Surely—"

"No, not 'surely,' because not one night in Paris, the city of love, not one night ever, did we make love!"

"There must have been—"

"No, not once. You've forgotten. I remember. Total recall. Never once, not once, did you call me to bed."

There was a long silence as she stared at the list and at last let it fall from her fingers. She did not look at him.

"Does it all come back now?" he wondered aloud.

She nodded silently.

"And isn't it sad?" he said.

She nodded again, quietly.

"Remember that lovely film we saw so long ago when Garbo and Melvyn Douglas looked at a clock in Paris and it was almost twelve and he says, 'Oh, Ninotchka, Ninotchka, the big hand and the little hand almost touch. Almost touch, and in a moment one half of Paris will be making love to the other half. Ninotchka, Ninotchka.' "

His wife nodded and a tear appeared in her eye.

He went to the door and opened it and said, "You do understand why I have to go? Because next year I might be too old, or maybe even not here."

"It's never too late—" she began.

"For us, yes, too late. Twenty years in Paris too late. Twenty weeks and twenty July 14 possible nights, Bastille Days, and all of it too late. My God it's sad. I could almost cry. But another year, I did. Good-bye."

"Good-bye," she whispered.

He opened the door and stood there, staring at the future.

"Oh, Ninotchka, Ninotchka," he whispered and went out and was careful to shut the door with no sound.

The concussion thrust her back in her chair.

THE TRANSFORMATION

1948–1949

BEFORE STEVE MOVED from his chair they had burst into the room, seized him, clapping a hand over his mouth, and now they carried him, limp with terror, out of the small yellow apartment. He saw the cracked ceiling plaster pass over him. Twisting his head violently he broke his mouth free, and, instantly, as they struggled him out the door, he saw the walls of his retreat, thumbtacked with pictures of strong men from *Strength and Health* and, on the floor, wildly strewn by the brief fight, the copies of *Flash Detective* he had been reading when their footsteps sounded outside his door.

He hung like a dead man between the four of them now. For a long time he was so sick with fear that he couldn't move, he was a dead weight they carried out into the night air. And Steve thought, This is all wrong, this is the South, I'm white, they're white, and they've come to my place and grabbed me. This can't be. Things like this don't happen. What's wrong with the world when a thing like this can happen?

The sweating palm clung to his mouth as they jolted him drunkenly across the lawn. He heard a casual laughing voice say, "Evening, Miss Landriss. It's our friend Steve Nolan. Drunk again, ma'am. Yes, *ma'am*!" And everybody laughed their pretending laughs.

He was thrown into the back of a car, and the men plunged in around him, pressing him among them like something closed into the pages of a book on a hot summer evening. The car lurched away from the curb, and then the voices were talking, and the hand came away from Steve Nolan's mouth so he could lick his lips and look at them with jittering, glassy eyes.

"Wh-what you going to do?" he gasped, stiffening his legs against the floorboards, as if to stop the car by this action.

"Stevie, Stevie." One of the men shook his head slowly.

"What you want with me?" cried Steve.

"You know what we want, Stevie boy."

"Let me out of here!"

"Hold on to him!"

They rushed down a country road in the dark. Crickets sounded on both sides and there was no moon, only a great number of stars in the black warm air.

"I didn't do nothing. I know you. You're them damned liberals, you're them Communists! You going to kill me!"

"We wouldn't think of doing that," said one of the men, patting Steve's cheek with a deadly soft pat, affectionate.

"Me," said another. "I'm a Republican. What are you, Joe?"

"Me? I'm a Republican too."

They both smiled cat-smiles at Steve. He was very cold. "If it's about that nigger woman Lavinia Walters—"

"Who said anything about Lavinia Walters?"

Everybody looked at everybody else, so surprised.

"You know anything about Lavinia Walters, Mack?"

"No, you?"

"Well, I heard tell something about how she had a kid recently. Is that the one you mean?"

"Now, now, look, boys, look, stop the car, stop the car, and I'll tell you all about this Lavinia Walters—" Steve's tongue moved, trembling over his lips. His eyes were frozen wide. His face was the color of clean bone. He looked like a corpse propped between the sweating, pressing men, out of place, ridiculous, gaunt with fear.

"Look here, why just look here!" he cried, laughing shrilly. "We're southerners, all of us, and we southerners got to stick together, now ain't that right? I mean now, ain't that the truth!"

"We *are* sticking together." The men looked at one another. "Aren't we, boys?"

"Wait a minute." Steve squinted at them. "I know you. You're

Mack Brown, you drive a truck for that carnival down at the creek. And you, you're Sam Nash, you work the carnival too. All of you from the carnival, and all local boys, you shouldn't be acting this way. Why, it's just the summer night. Now, you just park at that next crossroads and let me out and, by God, I won't say nothing about this to nobody." He smiled with wild generosity at them. "I *know*. Hot blood and all. But we're all from the same place, and who's that up in the front seat with Mack?"

A face turned in the dim cigarette light.

"Why, you're—"

"Bill Colum. Hello, Steve."

"Bill, I went to school with *you*!"

Colum's face was hard in the windy light. "I never did like you, Steve. And now I don't like you at all."

"If this is all over Lavinia Walters, that damn nigger woman, it's silly. I didn't do nothing to her."

"Nothing you haven't done to a dozen others over the years."

Mack Brown, up front, at the steering wheel, drooped his cigarette in his trap mouth. "I'm ignorant, I forget. What about this Lavinia, tell me, I'd like to hear it again."

"She was a nervy, goddamn sort of colored woman," said Sam, in the backseat, holding Steve. "Why, she even had the goddamn nerve to walk down Main Street yesterday carrying a little child in her arms. And you know what she was saying, Mack, out loud, so all the white folks could hear? She says, 'This is the child of Steve Nolan'!"

"Wasn't that *dirty* of her?"

They took a side road now, off toward the carnival grounds, over bumpy road.

"That ain't all. She went in every store where a Negro had never been in years, and she stood among the people and said, 'Looky here, this is Steve Nolan's baby. Steve Nolan.' "

The sweat was pouring down Steve's face. He began to fight. Sam just squeezed his throat hard and Steve quieted. "Go on with the story," said Mack, in the front seat.

"The way it all happened was Steve was ambling along the country road one afternoon in his Ford when he saw the prettiest colored girl, Lavinia Walters, walking along. And he stopped the car and told her if she didn't get in he'd tell the police she stole his wallet. And she was afraid, so she let him drive her off into the swamp for an hour."

"Is *that* what happened?" Mack Brown drew up beside the carnival tents. Being Monday night, the carnival was dead, unlit, the tents flapped softly in a warm wind. Somewhere a few dim blue lanterns burned, throwing ghastly lights on huge sideshow signs.

Sam Nash's hand moved before Steve's face, patting his cheeks, pinching and testing his chin, pinching the flesh on Steve's arms gently, approvingly. And for the first time, in the blue light, Steve saw the tattoos on Sam's hands, and he knew the tattoos went up the arms and all over Sam's body, he was the Carnival Tattoo Man. And as they sat there, the car silent, the trip over, all of them drenched with sweat, waiting, Sam finished the story.

"Well, Steve here made Lavinia meet him twice a week in the swamp, or else he'd turn her in, he said. She knew she was colored and wouldn't have much chance against a white man's word. And so yesterday she had the unmitigated nerve to walk down the main street of the town saying to everybody, *everybody,* mind you, this here is Steve Nolan's baby!"

"There's a woman ought to be hanged." Mack Brown turned and looked back at the men in the rear seat.

"She *was,* Mack," Sam assured him. "But we're ahead of our story. After she went through town saying that bad thing to everybody, she stopped right in front of Simpson's Grocery, right by the porch, you know, where all the men sit, and there was that rain barrel there. And she took her baby and pushed it down under the water, watching the bubbles come up. And she said, one last time, 'This is Steve Nolan's child.' Then she turned and walked off, with nothing in her hands."

That was the story.

Steve Nolan waited for them to shoot him. Cigarette smoke idled through the car.

"I—I had nothing to do with her being hung last night," said Steve.

"*Was* she hung?" asked Mack.

Sam shrugged. "She was found this morning in her shack by the river. Some say she committed suicide. Others say somebody visited her and strung her up to make it look like suicide. Now, Steve—" Sam tapped him softly on the chest. "Which story do *you* think's the right one?"

"She hung herself!" screamed Steve.

"Shh. Not so loud. We can hear you, Steve." Gently.

"We kind of figure, Steve," said Bill Colum. "You got pretty mad when she had the nerve to call your name and drown your baby on Main Street. So you fixed her for good and thought nobody would ever bother you."

"You should be ashamed." Steve had his false bravado up now, suddenly. "You're no real southerner, Sam Nash. Let go of me, goddamn it."

"Steve, let me tell you something." And Sam ripped all the buttons off Steve's white shirt with one twist of his hand. "We're a damn queer kind of southerners. We don't happen to like your kind. We been watching and thinking about you a long time, Steve, and tonight we couldn't stand thinking about you no more." He tore the rest of the shirt off Steve.

"You going to whip me?" said Steve, looking at his bare chest.

"No. Something far better than that." Sam jerked his head. "Bring him in the tent."

"No!" But he was yanked out and dragged into a dark tent, where a light was pulled on. Shadows swayed on all sides. They strapped him on a table and stood smiling with their thoughts. Over him, Steve saw a sign. TATTOOS! ANY DESIGN, ANY COLOR! And he began to get sick.

"*Guess* what I'm going to do to you, Steve?" Sam rolled up

his sleeves, showing the long red snakes printed on his hairy arms. There was a tinkle of instruments, a sound of liquid being stirred. The faces of the men looked down upon Steve with benevolent interest. Steve flickered his eyes and the TATTOOS sign wavered and dissolved in midair, in the warm tent. Steve stared at that sign and did not look away. TATTOOS. Any color. TATTOOS. Any color.

"No!" he screamed. "No!" But they unloosened his leg straps and cut his pants off with a pair of shears. He lay naked.

"But *yes*, Steve, yes indeed."

"You *can't* do that!"

He knew what they were going to do. He began to shriek.

Quietly, mildly, Sam applied some adhesive tape over Steve's lips just after Steve screamed, "Help!"

Steve saw the bright silver tattooing needle in Sam's hand.

Sam bent over him, intimately. He spoke earnestly and quietly, as if telling a secret to a small child. "Steve, here's what I'm going to do to you. First, I'm going to color your hands and arms, black. And then I'm going to color your body, black. And then I'll color your legs black. And then, finally, I'm going to tattoo your face, Steve, my friend. Black. The blackest black there ever was, Steve. Black as ink. Black as night."

"Mmmm." Steve shrieked inside the adhesive. The scream came out his nostrils, muffled. His lungs pumped the scream, his heart pumped it.

"And when we're done with you tonight," said Sam, "you

can just go home and pack your clothes and move on out of your apartment. Nobody'll want a black man living there. Regardless of how you got that way, Steve. Now, now, don't shake; it won't hurt much. I can just see you, Steve, moving over to nigger town, maybe. Living by yourself. Your landlord won't keep you on; his new tenants might think you were a nigger, lying about your skin. Landlord can't afford to risk tenants, so out you go. Maybe you can go north. Get a job. Not a job like you got now: ticket agent at the railway, no. But maybe a redcap job or a shoe-shine boy job, right, Steve?"

The scream again. Vomit erupted in two jets from Steve's nostrils. "Rip off the tape!" said Sam, "or he'll drown himself."

The adhesive came off, biting.

When Steve was through being sick, they replaced the tape.

"It's late." Sam glanced at his watch. "We'd better start if we want to finish with this."

The men leaned in over the table, their faces wet. There was a humming electric sound of the needle purring.

"Wouldn't it be a joke," said Sam, high up over Steve, pressing the needle onto Steve's naked chest, sewing it with black ink, "if Steve got shot for rape someday?" He waved his hand at Steve. "So long, Steve. See you in the back section of a streetcar!"

The voices faded. Deep inside, as Steve closed his eyes, he was wailing. And he heard the voices murmuring in the summer night, he saw Lavinia Walters walking down a street somewhere in the past, a child in her arms, he saw bubbles rising, and something hanging from a rafter, and he felt the needle gnawing and gnawing at his skin, forever and forever. He squeezed his eyes tight to fight his panic, and suddenly he knew only two very clear, certain things: tomorrow he must buy a pair of new white gloves to cover his hands. And then? Then he would break every mirror in his apartment.

He lay on the table, crying all night long.

SIXTY-SIX

2003

I'M GOING TO TELL YOU a story and you're not going to believe it, but nevertheless I'm going to tell you. It's kind of a murder mystery. On the other hand, maybe it's a time-travel story, and come to think of it, it's also a story of vengeance, and then throw in a couple of ghosts and there you have it.

What I am is a motorcycle officer with the Oklahoma police on what used to be called Route 66, somewhere between Kansas and Oklahoma City. During the last month a series of very strange discoveries has been made along the route from Kansas City to Oklahoma.

I discovered the bodies of a man, a woman, a younger man, and two children in fields along the way in early October. The bodies were widely distributed over an area of more than a hundred miles, and yet the way they were dressed indicated to me that, somehow, they were all related. Each of the bodies appeared to have died from some sort of strangulation, but that has not been definitively ascertained. There are no marks on the bodies, but all indications were that they were slain and left not far from the road.

The clothes they wore did not belong to this day in this month, in this year. Indeed, the clothing was not at all like what you'd buy at shops today.

The man appeared to be a farmer, dressed in work clothes: denims, a ragged shirt and battered hat.

The woman resembled a timeworn scarecrow, starved by life.

The younger man was dressed as a farmer also, but with clothes that looked like they had traveled five hundred miles in a dust storm.

The two children, a boy and a girl around twelve, also looked as if they had wandered the roads in heavy rains and blistering sun and then fallen by the way.

When I hear the phrase "Dust Bowl," memories come back that are not mine. My mother and father were born in the early 1920s and were alive during the Great Depression, which I heard about all my life. We people here in the center of America suffered that nightmare, which we've all seen in motion pictures—dust blowing in great billowing gusts across the land, destroying the barns and leveling the crops.

I've heard the story and seen it so often that I feel I lived through it. That is one of the reasons why my finding the bodies of these people was so strange.

I woke some nights ago around three in the morning and found that I had been crying and I didn't know why. I sat up in bed and realized I'd been dreaming about those bodies found all along the road, from Kansas City to the Oklahoma border.

It was then that I got up and rifled through some old books left to me by my parents and found pictures of the Okies: people who had gone west and who had been memorialized in Steinbeck's *Grapes of Wrath*. The more I looked at the pictures, the more I felt the need to weep. I had to put the books away and go back to bed, but I lay there for a long time with tears streaming down my face and only slept when the sun rose in the morning.

I've taken the long way to tell you about this because it has been so hurtful to my soul.

I found the body of the older man in an empty cornfield, strewn in a ditch, his clothes burnt by the sun and parched as in a dry harvest. I called in the county coroner and continued searching; I had an uneasy sense that there were more bodies to be found. Why I should think this still remains an immense mystery to me.

I found the woman thirty miles farther on, under a culvert, and she, in turn, bore no marks of violence but seemed dead as if from an invisible bolt of lightning having struck her in the night.

Fifty miles still farther on lay the bodies of the children and the young man.

When they were all assembled, like a jigsaw puzzle, in the county coroner's office, we surveyed them with a terrible sense of loss, though we did not know these people. Somehow we felt we had seen them before and known them well, and we mourned their deaths.

This entire case might have remained a terrible mystery forever. Many weeks later, as I waited for a haircut in a barbershop one afternoon, I leafed through a pile of magazines. Opening an issue of an old magazine, I came to a page of photographs that caused me to jump up, throw the magazine against the wall, then pick it up again, shouting to nobody, "Damn! Oh, Jesus! Damn!"

I clenched the magazine in my hand and stormed out.

Because, my God, the pictures of the Okies in the magazine were the same people I'd found along the road!

But, looking closer, I read that these pictures were taken weeks ago in New York, of folks dressed up to look like Okies.

The clothes they wore were new but made to look dusty and worn, and if you wanted to have them you could go to a department store and buy these old clothes at new prices and think yourself back sixty years.

I don't know what happened next. I kind of went redhot bloodshot blind. I heard someone yelling, and it was me. "Damn! Oh God!"

Crushing the magazine, I stared at my motorcycle.

The night was cold, and somehow I knew I had to ride my cycle somewhere. I rode off in the autumn weather for a long while and stopped every once in a while. I didn't know where I was, and I didn't care.

Now I'll tell you another thing that you won't believe, but when I'm done, maybe you will.

Have you ever been in a really big windstorm? The kind of storm that came through Kansas and blew over Oklahoma all those years of the Dust Bowl. When you see the photos and hear the name there is hardly any way for you to imagine how it was when the people inside the great wind couldn't see the horizon, didn't even know what time it was. The wind blew so hard it flattened farms, tore off roofs, knocked over windmills. It ruined a lot of poor roads, which were already nothing more than red mud.

Anyway, you get lost in the middle of a storm like that, when the dust burns your eyes and fills your ears, and you forget what day it is or what year and you wonder if something awful is going to happen and then maybe it's not awful, but it does happen and it's there.

This big wind roared up and I was on the road on my motorbike when it hit. I had to stop my bike I was so blind. I stood there with the sun going down beyond the storm and the wind howling and I was afraid for the first time. I didn't know what I was afraid of, but I waited with my motorbike and after a long while the wind sort of died, and coming along Route 66 from the eastern horizon, going real slow, was an old jalopy;

an open car with bundles in the back and a water bag on the side, and steam coming out of the radiator and dirt crusted over the windshield so whoever was driving had to half stand to look over to see the road.

The car puttered up close to me and then sort of ran out of gas. The man behind the wheel looked at me and I looked at him. He was tall, even sitting in his seat, and his face was bony and his hands were bony on the wheel. There was a crumpled hat on his head, and he had a three-day beard. His eyes looked like he'd been in a night storm forever.

He waited for me to speak.

I walked over and all I could say was "You lost?"

He looked at me with his steady gray eyes. His head didn't move, but his lips did. "No, not now. Is this the Dust Bowl?"

I sort of pulled back and then I said, "I haven't heard those words since I was a kid. Yeah, this is it."

"And this is Route 66?"

I nodded.

"That's how I figured," he said. "Well, if I go straight on, will I get where I want to go?"

"Where's that?"

He looked at my uniform and his shoulders sort of sagged. "I was looking for, I think, a police station."

"Why?" I said.

"Because," he said, "I think I want to give myself up."

"Well, maybe you can give yourself up to me. But why would you want to do that?"

"Because," he said, "I think I killed some folks."

I looked back down the road to where the dust was settling. "Back there?" I said.

He looked over his shoulder very slowly and nodded. "Yup, back there." The wind went high again and the dust was thick.

"How long ago?" I said.

He closed his eyes. "Some time during the last few weeks."

"Folks?" I said. "Killed? How many?"

He opened his eyes and his eyelashes quivered. "Four, no, five. Yeah, five people, dead now. Good riddance. Do I give myself up to you?"

I hesitated because something was wrong. "This is too easy. You've got to say more."

"Well," he said, "I don't know how to tell you, but I've been driving this road for a long time. Gotta be years."

Years, I thought. That's how I felt too, that he'd been driving for years.

"And then what?" I said.

"These people sort of got in the way. One of them looked like my pa and the other looked like my ma when she was very young and the third one looked like my brother, but he's long dead. I used to have another brother and sister, and they were there too. It was so damned strange."

"Five people?" I said. And my mind went back to the days behind and the five people I'd found on the road between Kansas City and Oklahoma. "Five?"

He nodded. "That's it."

"Well," I said, "what had they done? Why would you want to kill them?"

"They was just on the road," he said. "I don't know how they got there, but the way they dressed and the way they looked, I knew something was wrong and I had to stop and fix each one, make them drop forever. I just had to do it." He looked at his hands on the steering wheel, which were clenched tight.

"Hitchhikers?" I said.

"Not exactly," he said. "Something worse. Hitchhikers are okay, they're going somewhere. But these folks, they were just poachers I guess. Claim jumpers, criminals, robbers of some sort. It's hard to say." He looked back down the road again where the dust was beginning to stir up just a bit.

"Do you ever come out of church Sunday noon, feeling clean, like you had another chance for who knows what, and you stand there, reborn, with folks happy unto joy, as the preacher says, and then in the midst of noon folks from across town drive up in their dark suits and undertake you, I mean undertake your happiness with their demon smiles, and you stand there with your folks and feel the joy just melt away like a spring thaw and when they see they've undertook your joy they drive away in their own kind of sinful undertaking of happiness?"

The driver stopped, added up the sums inside his eyelids, and at last let his breath out. "Ain't that a sort of, I don't know, kind of—" He searched and found the word. "Blasphemy?"

I waited, thought, and said, "That's the word."

"We weren't doing nothing, just standing there, fresh out of the revival, and they just came by and undertook us."

"Blasphemy," I said.

"I was only ten, but that was the first time in my life I wanted to grab a hoe and rake their smiles. And you stand there, feeling naked. They've stolen your Sunday best. Don't you think I got a right to just say give back, hand over, I'll take that coat, shuck off those pants and the hat too, yeah, the hat?"

"Five people," I said. "An older man, a woman, a younger man, and two kids. That sounds familiar."

"Then you know what I'm saying. They were wearing those clothes. It's funny, the clothes they were wearing, it looked like they had been through the Dust Bowl, stayed there a long time, and maybe lived out in the open and slept at night with the wind blowing and their clothes getting full of dust and their faces sort of getting thin and I looked at each one and I said to the older man, 'You're not my pa.' And the old man couldn't answer. I looked at the woman and said, 'You're not my ma,' and she didn't answer either. And I looked at my brother and my other younger brother and sister and said, 'I don't know any of you. You look right, but you feel wrong. What are you doing on this road?' Well, they didn't say anything. They was kind of, I don't know, ashamed maybe, but they wouldn't get out of the way. They were standing in front of the car, and I knew if I didn't do something they wouldn't let me go on to Oklahoma City. So you know what I did?"

"Put a stop to them," I said.

"*Stop* is a good word. Yank off the clothes, I thought to myself. They don't deserve to have those clothes. Take away their skin, I thought, because they don't deserve to look like my mom and dad and brothers and sister. So I sort of edged the car forward, but they didn't move and they couldn't speak because they was ashamed and the wind came up and I moved the car. As I moved, they fell down in front of it and I drove straight on and when I looked back I hoped the bottom of the car had ripped their clothes off, but no, they were still full dressed, which they didn't deserve, and they were lying there on the road, and if they was dead I wasn't sure, but I hoped they was. I got out and went back and one by one I picked them up, put them in the back of the car, and I took off down the road with the dust rising and I laid them out here and there and somewhere else, and by that time they didn't look like any of my folks at all. That's a peculiar story, don't you figure?"

"It's peculiar," I said.

"Well then," he said, "that's it. I've told it all. You gonna take me in?"

I looked into his face and looked down the road and I thought of the bodies still lying in the coroner's office in Topeka. "I'll think about it," I said.

"What do you mean?" he said. "I've told it all. I'm guilty. I did them in."

I waited. The wind and the dust were rising even more. I

said, "No. Strange, I don't think you're guilty. Don't know why, but I don't think you are."

"Well, it's getting late," he said. "You want to see my identification?"

"If you want to show it," I said.

He pulled a battered wallet out of his pocket and handed it over. There was no driver's license, just an old card with a name on it I couldn't quite read, but it looked familiar, something out of the newspapers long before I was born. The back of my neck got real cold and I said, "Where you heading after this?"

"I don't know," he said. "But I'm feeling better than when I started the trip. What's ahead up there on the road?"

"Same as always," I said. "California, postcards, oranges, lemons, maybe government camps, bungalow courts." I handed him back his card and wallet. "There's a police station about ten miles ahead. By the time you get there, if you still feel you've gotta give yourself up, do it there, but I'm not your man."

"How come?" he said, his eyes quiet and gray and steady.

"All I know is sometimes some people don't deserve to wear the clothes that they wear or wear the faces that they got. Some people," I said at last, "get in the way."

"I drove real slow," he said.

"And they didn't move."

"Right," he said. "I just went right over them and that was it and I felt good. Well, I guess I better be gettin' on."

I stood back and let the car drift. It went down the road, the driver hunched over the wheel, his hands on the steering wheel and the dust following him as he got smaller in the twilight.

I stood watching him for the next five minutes until he was gone. By that time the wind was rising and the dust was filling my eyes. I couldn't tell where I was or if I was crying. I went back to my motorcycle, got on, hit the throttle, and turned around and went the other way.

a MATTER OF TASTE

1952

I WAS NEAR THE SKY when the silver ship flew down to us. I drifted through the high trees on the great morning web and all my friends came with me. Our days were always the same and always good and we were happy. But we were also happy to see the silver carrier drop from space. For it meant a new but not unreasonable change in our tapestry, and we felt we could adjust to the pattern, even as we had adjusted to all the ravelings and unravelings of a million years.

We are an old and a wise race. We considered space travel at one time and gave it up, for it meant that the refinement we were seeking in our own lives would be torn like a web in a storm, and a one-hundred-thousand-year philosophy interrupted just when it was bearing the ripest and most agreeable fruit. We decided to stay here on our rain and jungle world and live peacefully at ease.

But now—this silver craft from the heavens gave us a stir of quiet adventure. For here came travelers from some other planet who had chosen a course diametrically opposed to ours. The night, they say, has much to teach the day, and the sun, they continue, may light the moon. So I went happily, my friends went happily, in a glide, in a pleasant dream, down toward the jungle clearing where lay the silver carrier.

I must describe the afternoon: the great web cities glittered with cool rain, the trees freshly rinsed with falling waters, and now the sun bright. I had partaken of an especially succulent meal, the good wine of the humming jungle-bee, and a warm languor tempered and made my excitement all the more enjoyable.

But—a curious thing: while all of us, numbering perhaps a thousand, gathered about the craft in friendly demeanor and attitude, the ship did nothing, it remained firmly unto itself. Its portals did not open. Momentarily, I thought I glimpsed some creature at a small port above, but perhaps I was mistaken.

"For some reason," I said to my friends, "the inhabitants of this beautiful craft are not venturing forth."

We discussed this. We decided that perhaps—the reasoning of animals from other worlds being possibly of a divergent nature from our own—that perhaps they felt somewhat outnumbered by our welcoming committee. This seemed doubtful, but nevertheless I transmitted this sentiment to the others about us, and in less than a second the jungle trembled, the great golden webs shivered, and I was left alone by the ship.

I then advanced, in a breath, to the port and said aloud: "We welcome you to our cities and lands!"

I was soon pleased to note that some machinery was working within the ship. After a minute the portway opened.

No one appeared.

I called out in a friendly voice.

Ignoring me, a conversation was in rapid progress inside the ship. I understood none of it, naturally, for it was in a foreign tongue. But the essence of it was bewilderment, some little anger, and a tremendous, and to me strange, fear.

I have a precise memory. I remember that conversation, which meant nothing, which still means nothing to me. The words stand in my mind now. I need only pluck them and give them to you:

"*You* go out, Freeman!"

"No, *you*!"

A bumble of indecision, a mixing of apprehension, followed. I was on the point of repeating my friendly invitation when a single creature picked its way carefully from the ship and stood looking up at me.

Curious. The creature shook in mortal fear.

I was much concerned, immediately. I could not understand this senseless panic. Certainly I am a mild and honorable individual. I bore this visitor no malice; indeed, the machinery of malice last rustled long ago on our world. Yet here the creature was, pointing what I understood to be a metal weapon at me, and trembling. The thought of killing was in the creature's mind.

I immediately soothed him.

"I am your friend," I said and repeated it, as a thought, as an emotion. I put the warmness in my mind, a love, and a promise of a long and happy life, and this I sent to the visitor.

Well, where it had not responded to my spoken word, it responded, visibly, to my telepathy. It—relaxed.

"Good," I heard it say. That was the word. I recall it exactly. A meaningless word, but the creature's mind was warmer behind the symbol.

You will forgive me if here I describe my guest.

It was quite small. I would say only six feet tall, with a head on a short stalk, only four limbs, two of which it used exclusively, it seemed, for walking, while the other two were not used for walking at all, but simply *held* things, or gestured! It was with a flush of amusement I noted the lack of another set of limbs, so necessary to us, so useful. Yet this creature seemed perfectly at ease with its body, so I accepted it in the same sense that it accepted itself.

The pale-colored creature, almost hairless, had features of a most peculiar aesthetic, the mouth particularly, while the eyes were sunken and of a surprising art, like the noon sea. All in all, it was a strange work, and as a curiosus, as a new adventure, quite exciting. It challenged my taste and my philosophy.

I made the adjustment instantaneously.

I thought such thoughts as these to my new friend:

"We are all your fathers and your children. We welcome you to our great tree cities, to our cathedral life, to our quiet customs, and to our thoughts. You will move in peace among us. You need not fear."

I heard it say aloud, "My God! Monstrous! A spider, seven feet tall!"

It was then seized with some sort of spell, some paroxysm. Fluid gushed from its mouth, it shuddered violently.

I felt compassion and pity and sadness. Something was making this poor creature ill. It fell down, its face, which was white, was now very white indeed. It was gasping and trembling.

I moved to give it aid. In doing so, I must have somehow alarmed those within the ship by my speed, for even as I plucked up the fallen creature to render it help, an inner door of the ship flung wide. Others like my friend leaped out, shouting, confused, frightened, waving silver weapons.

"He's got Freeman!"

"Don't shoot! Idiot, you'll hit Freeman!"

"Careful!"

"God!"

Those were the words. Meaningless even now, but remembered. I felt the fear in them, however. It burned the air. It burned my brain.

I have a mind of quick thinking. Instantly, I rushed forward, deposited the creature where he would be in easy reach of the others, and retreated soundlessly from their climate, thinking back at them: "He is yours. He is my friend. You are all my friends. All is well. I would help you and him, if I may. He is ill. Take fine care of him."

They were amazed. They stood, and their thought was amazement and a species of shock. They vanished their friend within the ship and stood gazing out and up at me. I sent my friendship, like a warm sea wind, to them. I smiled upon them.

Then I returned to the city of jeweled web, to our good city among the high trees, under the sun, in the fresh sky. It was beginning to rain a new rain. As I reached the place of my children and my children's children, I heard some words from far below and saw the creatures stand in the portway of their ship, looking up at me. The words were these:

"Friendly, by God. Friendly spiders."

"How can that be?"

Feeling very well, I started this tapestry and this narration, using wild lime-plums and peaches and oranges strung upon golden web. It made a fine pattern.

A NIGHT PASSED. The cool rains fell and washed our cities and hung them with clear jewels. I said to my friends, let the craft lie there alone, let the creatures therein accustom themselves to our world, they will venture out farther, at last, and we will be friends, and their fear will vanish as all fears must, with love and friendship present. There will be much for our two cultures to learn. They, new, and boldly venturing into space in metal seeds, and us, very old and comfortable and hanging in our cities at midnight, feeling the rain fall upon us benevolently. We will teach them the philosophy of wind and stars and how the green grows up and how the sky is when it is blue and warm at noon. Surely they will want to know this. And they, in turn, will refresh us with tales of their far planet, perhaps even of their wars and conflicts, to remind us of our own past and what we, with common sense, have put away, like evil toys, in the sea. Let them be, friends, patience. In a few days, all will be well.

IT WAS CERTAINLY OF INTEREST. The air of confusion and horror that lay over that ship for a week. Again and again, from our comfortable sites in the trees, in the sky, we saw the creatures gazing at us. I put my mind into their ship and heard their words, unable to guess their meaning, but getting an emotional content, anyway:

"Spiders! My God!"

"Big ones! Your turn to go out, Negley."

"No, not me!"

It was on the afternoon of the seventh day that one of the creatures came forth, alone, unarmed, and called up to me in the sky. I called back and sent him friendship, warmly, and with good intent. In an instant, the great jeweled city was trembling behind me in the sun. I stood by the visitor.

I should have known better. He broke and ran.

I pulled up short, continually sending my best and kindest thoughts. He calmed and returned. I sensed that they had had some sort of volunteering or contest. And this creature had been picked.

"Do not tremble," I thought.

"No," he thought, in my own language.

It was my turn to be surprised, but delighted.

"I've learned your language," he said, aloud, slowly, his eyes turning wildly, his mouth shaking. "With machines. During the week. You *are* friendly, aren't you?"

"Of course." I squatted, so we were on an equal level, eye to eye. We were perhaps six feet apart. He kept edging away. I smiled. "What do you fear? Not me, surely?"

"Oh, no, no," he said, hastily.

I heard his heart thumping in the air, a drum, a warm murmur, quick and deep.

In his mind, without knowing that I could read it, he thought, using our language: "Well, if I'm killed, the ship will only be out one man. Better lose one, than all."

"Kill!" I cried, shocked by the thought, stunned and amused. "Why, nobody has died in violence on our world for one hundred thousand years. Please put the thought away. We shall be friends."

The creature swallowed. "We've been studying you with instruments. Telepathy machines. Various gauges," he said. "You have a civilization here?"

"As you see," I said.

"Your IQ," he said, "has astounded us. From what we see and hear, it is above two hundred."

The term was a trifle ambiguous, but, again, of a fine humor to me, and I gave him a thought of joy and pleasure. "Yes," I said.

"I am the captain's aide," said the creature, venturing what I learned to be his own smile. The difference being, note, he smiled horizontally, instead of on the vertical, as do we members of the city of the trees.

"Where is the captain?" I asked.

"Ill," he replied. "Ill since the day of arrival."

"I'd like to meet him," I said.

"I'm afraid that won't be possible."

"I'm sorry to hear that," I said. I sent my mind into the ship, and there was the captain, stretched out upon a kind of bed, muttering. Very sick indeed. He cried out from time to time. He shut his eyes and warded off a kind of fevered vision. "Oh, God, God," he kept saying, in his own tongue.

"Your captain is afraid of something?" I asked politely.

"No, no, oh, no," said the aide, nervously. "Just sick. We've had to select a new captain who'll come out later." He edged off. "Well, I'll see you."

"Let me escort you about our city tomorrow," I said. "All are welcome."

As he stood there, all the time he stood there talking to me, this awful trembling moved in him. Trembling, trembling, trembling, trembling.

"You are sick, also?" I asked.

"No, no," he said, turned, and ran into the ship.

Inside the ship, I felt him to be very sick.

I returned to our city in the heavens, among the trees, sorely perplexed. "How odd," I said. "How nervous these visitors are."

At twilight, as I continued work upon this plum and orange tapestry, I heard the one word drift up to me:

"Spider!"

But then I forgot this, for it was time to go up to the top of the city and wait for the first new wind off the sea, to sit there, among my friends, at peace, enjoying the smell and the goodness of it all, through the night.

IN THE MIDDLE OF THE NIGHT, I said to the begetter of my fine children: "What is it? Why are they afraid? What is there to fear? Am I not a good creature of fine intelligence and friendly character?" And the answer was yes. "Then why the trembling, the sickness, the violent ailments?"

"Perhaps a suggestion of this is in their appearance to us," said my wife. "I find them odd."

"Admitted."

"And strange."

"Yes, of course."

"And a little frightening in appearance. Looking at them, I am somewhat uncomfortable. They are so different."

"Think it through, consider it intelligently, and such thoughts vanish," I said. "It's a matter of aesthetics. We're simply accustomed to us. We have eight legs, they only four, two of which are not used as legs at all. Odd, strange, momentarily unsettling, yes, but I adjusted immediately, with reason. Our aesthetic is resilient."

"Perhaps theirs is not. Perhaps they do not like the way *we* look."

I laughed at this. "What, be frightened of just outward appearances? Nonsense!"

"You're right, of course. It must be something else."

"I wish I knew," I said. "I wish I knew. I wish I could put them at ease."

"Forget it," said my wife. "A new wind has arisen. Listen. *Listen.*"

THE NEXT DAY I took the new captain on a tour of our city. We talked for hours. Our minds met. He was a doctor of the mind. He was an intelligent creature. Less intelligent than we, yes. But this is nothing to consider with prejudice. I found him a creature of wit, good humor, considerable knowledge, and few prejudices, actually. Yet, all through the afternoon, while touring our heaven-moored city, I felt the hidden trembling, trembling.

I was too polite to mention it again.

The new captain swallowed a number of tablets from time to time.

"What are those?" I asked.

"For my nerves," he said, quickly. "That's all."

I carried him everywhere, and as often as possible I let him down to rest upon a tree branch. When it came time to go on again, he quailed when first I touched him and his face was terrible to see, in its own way.

"We are friends, aren't we?" I asked, with concern.

"Yes, friends. What?" He seemed to hear me for the first time. "Of course. Friends. You're a splendid race. This is a lovely city."

We talked of art and beauty and time and rain and the city. He kept his eyes shut. He kept his eyes shut and then we got on beautifully. Then he became excited when we talked and he laughed and was happy and complimented me on my own wit and intelligence. Strangely, I recall now that I got on best with him when I looked at the sky and not at him. This is an odd thing to note. He with his eyes closed, talking of minds and history and old wars and problems, and myself replying quickly.

It was only when he opened his eyes that he became almost instantly remote. I felt sad at this. He seemed to feel sad too. For he closed his eyes quickly and talked on, and in a minute our old rapport was reestablished. His trembling vanished.

"Yes," he said, eyes shut, "we are very good friends indeed."

"I am happy to hear you say that," I said.

I took him back to the ship. We bade each other good night, but he was trembling again and he went inside the ship and could not eat his evening meal. This I knew, for my mind was there. And I returned to my family, excited by a day intelligently spent, but colored by a sadness I had never known.

MY TALE IS almost at an end. The ship stayed with us another week. I saw the captain each day. We had wonderful times, talking, he with his face averted or his eyes closed. Our two worlds would get on well, he said. I agreed. All would be done in a great spirit of friendship. I toured various members of the crew through the city, but some became so stunned, for one reason or another, that I returned them, with apologies, in shock, to the spacecraft. All of them looked thinner than when they had landed. All had nightmares at night. The nightmares drifted to me, in a hot mist, very late, in darkness.

I record now a conversation I heard, by my mind, among the various members of that ship, on the last night. It is entirely by rote, with my incredible memory, that I set down these words, which mean nothing but may, someday, mean something to my descendants. Perhaps I am somewhat at disease. I feel a bit unhappy tonight for some reason. For there are still thoughts of death and terror in that ship below. I do not know what tomorrow will bring, surely I do not believe these creatures mean us harm. In spite of their thoughts, so tortured and in confusion. I put this conversation of theirs into tapestry, however, in the event that some unbelievable incident should occur. I shall hide the tapestry in a deep burial mound in the forest for posterity. The conversation went, then, like this:

"What'll we do, Captain?"

"About them? About them?"

"The spiders, the spiders. What'll we *do*?"

"I don't know. God, I've tried to figure it. They're friendly. They have *fine* minds. They are *good*. This is no evil plot of theirs. I'm positive that if we wanted to move in, use their minerals, sail their seas, fly in their sky, they would welcome us with love and charity."

"We *all* agree, Captain."

"But when I *think* of bringing my wife and children—"

A shuddering.

"It would never work."

"Never."

Trembling, trembling.

"I can't face going out again tomorrow. I can't stand another day of being with those things."

"When I was a boy, I remember, a barn, a spider—"

"Jesus!"

"But we're men, aren't we, strong men? Don't we have any guts? What are we, *cowards*?"

"This isn't reason. It's instinct, aesthetics, call it what you will. Will *you* go out tomorrow and talk to the Big One, that big hairy one with the eight legs, so damned tall?"

"No!"

"The captain's still in shock. None of us can eat. How would our children be, our wives, if *we* are this weak?"

"But they're *good*. They're *kind*. They're generous, they're everything we'll *never* be. They love everyone and they love us. They offer us help. They bid us enter."

"And enter we must, for many good reasons, commercial and otherwise."

"They're our *friends*!"

"Oh, God, yes."

Trembling, trembling, trembling.

"But it'll never work. They're just not *human*."

I am here in this night sky with my tapestry almost finished. I look forward to tomorrow when the captain will come again and we will talk. I look forward to the coming of all these good creatures who are confused now and somewhat alarmed but who will learn in time to love and be loved, to live with us and be our good friends. Tomorrow, the captain and I, I hope, will speak of rain and the sky and flowers and how it is when two creatures understand each other. The tapestry is finished. I finish it with a final quotation, in their own tongue, from the voices of the men in the ship, the voices that drift up to me on the blue night wind. Voices that seemed calmer and that accept circumstances and are not afraid anymore. Here ends my tapestry:

"You've decided then, Captain?"

"There's only *one* thing to do, sir."

"Yes. Only one possible thing to do."

"It's not POISONOUS*!" said the wife.*

"But!" The husband jumped up, raised his foot, stomped three times on the rug, shuddering.

He stood looking down at the wet spot on the floor.

His trembling stopped.

I Get the Blues When It Rains (A Remembrance)

1980

THERE IS ONE NIGHT in everyone's life that has to do with time and memory and song. It has to happen—it must spring up with spontaneity and die away when finished and never happen again quite the same. To try to make it happen only makes it fail. But when it does happen, it is so beautiful you remember it for the rest of your days.

Such a night happened to me and some writing friends, oh, thirty-five or forty years ago. It all began with a song titled "I Get the Blues When It Rains." Sound familiar? It should, to you older ones. To the younger, stop reading HERE. Most of what I have to offer from this point on belongs to a time before your birth and has to do with all the junk we put away in our attic heads and never take out until those special nights when memory prowls the trunks and unlocks the rusty hasps and lets out all the old and mediocre but somehow lovely words, or worthless but suddenly priceless tunes.

We had gathered at my friend Dolph Sharp's house in the Hollywood Hills for an evening of reading aloud our short stories, poetry, and novels. There that night were such writers as Sanora Babb, Esther McCoy, Joseph Petracca, Wilma Shore, and a half dozen others who had published their first stories or books in the late 1940s and early 1950s. Each arrived that evening with a new manuscript, primed to be read.

But a strange thing happened on the way across Dolph Sharp's front room.

Elliot Grennard, one of the senior writers of the group and a onetime jazz musician, passed the piano, touched the keys, paused, and played a chord. Then another chord. Then he laid his manuscript aside and put the bass in with his left hand and started playing an old tune.

We all looked up. Elliot glanced over at us and winked, standing there, letting the song play itself out nice and easy. "Know it?" he said.

"My God," I cried, "I haven't heard that in years!"

And I began to sing along with Elliot, and then Sanora came in and then Joe, and we sang: "I get the blues when it rains."

We smiled at one another and the words came louder: "The blues I can't lose when it rains."

We knew all the words and sang them and finished it and when we were done we laughed and Elliot sat down and rambled through "I Found a Million Dollar Baby in a Five and Ten Cent Store," and we discovered we all knew the words to that one too.

And then we sang "China Town, My China Town," and after that, "Singin' in the Rain"—yes, "singin' in the rain, what a glorious feelin', I'm happy again. . . ."

Then someone remembered "In a Little Spanish Town": " 'Twas on a night like this, stars were peek-a-booing down, 'Twas on a night like this. . . ."

And Dolph cut in with "I met her in Monterrey a long time ago, I met her in Monterrey, in old Mexico. . . ."

Then Joe yelled, "Yes, we have no bananas, we have no bananas today," which cut the sentiment for two minutes and led almost inevitably into "The Beer Barrel Polka" and "Hey, Mama, the Butcher Boy for Me."

No one remembers who brought out the wine, but someone did, and we didn't get drunk, no, we drank the wine, just the right amount, because the singing and the songs were everything. We were high on that.

We sang from nine until ten, at which time Joe Petracca said, "Stand aside, let the wop sing 'Figaro.' " And we did, and he did. We got very quiet, listening to him, for we discovered he had a more than ordinarily firm, sweet voice. All alone, Joe sang sections of *La Traviata*, a bit of *Tosca*, and finished off with "Un bel dì." He kept his eyes shut all the way to the end, then opened them, surprised, looked around and said, "For Christ's sake, it's getting too serious! Who knows 'By a Waterfall' from *Golddiggers of 1933*?"

Sanora did Ruby Keeler on that one, and someone else came in like Dick Powell. We were ransacking the house for more bottles by then, and Dolph's wife slipped out of the house and drove down the hill to bring up more booze, for we could tell if the songs went on, then the drinking would too.

We slid the long way back to "You were meant for me, I was meant for you. . . . Angels patterned you and when they were done, you were all the sweet things rolled up in one. . . ." By midnight we had worked through all the Broadway melodies old and new, half the 20th Century-Fox musicals, some Warner Bros., with bits and pieces of "Yes, sir, that's my baby, no, sir, I don't mean maybe," thrown in with "You're Blasé" and "Just a Gigolo," then fell off the deep end into all the old mammy songs, a baker's dozen of lousy sweet rolls that nevertheless we sang with fake tenderness. Everything bad sounded somehow good. Everything good was simply great. And everything that had always been wonderful was now superb beyond madness.

By one o'clock we had left the piano and sung our way out to the patio, where, a cappella, Joe tossed in more Puccini, and Esther and Dolph duetted on "Ain't she sweet, see her comin' down the street, now I ask you very confidentially. . . ."

From one-fifteen on, keeping our voices down, because the neighbors telephoned and said we should, it was Gershwin time. “I Love That Funny Face” and then “Puttin’ on the Ritz.”

By two we were into some champagne and suddenly remembered our parents’ songs sung in home cellars fixed up for birthday parties in 1928 or hummed on warm summer night porches when most of us were ten: “There’s a Long, Long Trail a-Winding into the Land of My Dreams.”

Then Esther remembered that her friend Theodore Dreiser had written the old favorite: “O the moon is bright tonight along the Wabash, from the fields there comes the scent of new-mown hay. Through the sycamores the candlelight is gleaming—on the banks of the Wabash, far away. . . .”

Then it was: “Nights are long since you went away. . . .”

And: “Smile the while I bid you sad adieu, when the years roll by I’ll come to you.”

And: “Jeanine, I dream of lilac time.”

And: “Gee, but I’d give the world to see that old gang of mine.”

And: “Those wedding bells are breaking up that old gang of mine.”

And finally, of course: “Should auld acquaintance be forgot. . . .”

By that time all the bottles were empty and we were back at “I Get the Blues When It Rains,” and the clock struck three and Dolph’s wife was standing by the open front door holding out our coats, which we went over to and put on and walked out into the night, still whisper-singing.

I don't remember who drove me home or how we got there. I only remember tears drying on my face because it had been a very special, very dear time, something that had never happened before and would never happen again in just that way.

The years have gone, Joe and Elliot are long since dead, the rest of us have grown somewhat beyond middle age, we have loved and lost in our careers and sometimes won, and we still meet on occasion and read our stories at Sanora's or Dolph's, with some new faces among us, and at least once a year we remember Elliot at the piano playing on that night we wanted to have go on forever, that night, which was loving and warm and fine, and all the sappy songs meant nothing but somehow meant everything. It was just as dumb and sweet, just as awful and lovely as Bogie saying, "Play it, Sam," and Sam playing and singing, "You must remember this, a kiss is just a kiss, a sigh is just a sigh. . . ."

It shouldn't work. It shouldn't be magic. You shouldn't weep happy and then sad and then happy again.

But you do. And I do. And we all do.

One last memory.

One night about two months after that special fine evening, gathered at the same house, Elliot came in and passed by the piano and stopped, eyeing it dubiously.

"Play 'I Get the Blues When It Rains,'" I said.

He played it.

It wasn't the same. The old night was gone forever. Whatever had been in that night was not in this. Same people, same place, same memories, same possible tunes, but . . . it had been special. It would always be special. Now, wisely, we turned away. Elliot sat down and picked up his manuscript. After a long moment of silence, glancing just once at the piano, Elliot cleared his throat and read us the title of his new short story.

I read next. While I was reading, Dolph's wife tiptoed behind us and quietly put the lid down on the piano.

ALL MY ENEMIES ARE DEAD

2003

THERE IT WAS ON PAGE SEVEN, the obituary: *Timothy Sullivan. Computer genius. 77. Cancer. Services private. Burial, Sacramento.*

"Oh God!" cried Walter Gripp. "Jesus, that does it, it's all over."

"What's all over?" I said.

"No use living. Read that." Walter shook the obituary.

"So?" I said.

"All of my enemies are dead."

"Hallelujah!" I laughed. "You've waited for that son of a bitch—"

"—bastard."

"Bastard, yes, for him to kick the bucket for a long time. Rejoice."

"Rejoice, hell. Now I got no reason, no reason to live."

"How's that again?"

"You don't understand. Tim Sullivan was a true son of a bitch. I hated him with all my blood, guts, and being."

"So?"

"You're not listening, I can tell. With him gone, the light has gone out." Walter's face grew pale.

"What light, dammit?!"

"The fire, dammit, in my chest, my heart, my ganglion. It lived off him. He kept me going. I went to sleep nights happy with hatred. I woke up mornings glad to breakfast on my need, my need to kill him all over again between lunch and dinner. But now he's spoiled it, blew out the flame."

"He did *that* to you? His last act was to provoke you with his death?"

"You might say that."

"I just did!"

"Now, let's get to bed and relapse my need."

"Don't be a sap, sit up and drink your gin. Now what are you doing?"

"As you see, pulling back the sheet. This may be my last lie-in."

"Get away from there, this is stupid."

"Death is stupid, an insult, dumb trick to die on me."

"So he did it on purpose?"

"I wouldn't put it past him. Just my kind of nasty. Call the mortuary, read me a menu of headstones, plain rock, no angels. Where are you going?"

"Outside. I need air."

"I may be gone by the time you're back!"

"Wait while I talk to someone sane!"

"Who's that?"

"Me!"

I went out and stood in the sun.

This can't be happening, I thought.

Oh no? I retorted. Go look.

Not yet. What'll we do?

Don't ask me, said my other self. If he dies, we die. No more work, no moola. Let's talk something else. Is that his address book?

That's it.

Flip through, there's got to be someone still alive and kicking.

Okay. I flipped. There go the *A*'s, the *B*'s and *C*'s! Dead! Check the *D*'s, *E*'s, *F*'s and *G*'s!

Dead!

I slammed the book shut, like the door of a tomb.

He was right: his friends, his enemies—it's a book of the dead.

That's colorful, write it down.

Colorful, Jesus! *Think* of something!

Hold on. How do I feel about him right now? That's it! Gangway! We're going back!

I opened the door and stuck my head in.

"Still dying?"

"What does it look like?"

"A stubborn ass."

I came in the door, walked in, and towered over him.

"Better close up?" said Walter.

"Not stubborn. Mean. Hold on while I gather my spit."

"I'm holding," said Walter. "Hurry up, I'm almost gone."

"Would that were true. Now listen up!"

"Don't stand so close, I can feel your breath."

"This is not mouth-to-mouth, just a reality check: now hear this!"

Walter blinked. "Is that my old chum, old pal?" A shadow crossed his face.

"No. Not old chum, old pal."

Walter beamed. "Sure, that's you, old buddy!"

"Since you're almost dead, it's time for a confession."

"I should be the one to confess."

"Me first!"

Walter closed his eyes and waited.

"Shoot," he said.

"Recall that missing cash back in '69, when you thought Sam Willis carried it to Mexico?"

"Yeah, Sam, sure."

"No. Me."

"How's that?"

"Me," I said. "I did it. Sam ran off with some babe. I snatched the moola and blamed him! Me!"

"That's not so bad," said Walter. "I forgive you."

"Hold on, there's more."

"I'm holding." Walter laughed, quietly.

"About that senior prom in high school, 1958."

"A wet-blanket night. I got Dica-Ann Frisbie. I needed Mary-Jane Caruso."

"You woulda had her. I told Mary-Jane all about your womanizing, listed your scores!"

"You did *that*!?" Walter opened his eyes wide. "So she wound up at the prom with you."

"That's it."

Walter fixed me with a brief stare, then looked away. "Well, hell, that's old water under an older bridge. You done?"

"Not quite."

"Jesus God! This is getting interesting. Spill it." Walter punched his pillow and reared up on one elbow.

"Then there was Henrietta Jordan."

"My God, Henrietta. What a beaut. That was a great summer."

"I ended that summer."

"You *what*?!"

"She dropped you, yes? Said her mother was dying, had to spend time with Mom."

"Then you ran off with Henrietta too?"

"That's it. Next item: remember when I got you to sell Ironworks, Inc., at a loss? Next week I bought on the way up."

"That's not so bad." Walter swallowed.

I went on. "Item: In Barcelona, '69, I pleaded migraine, went to bed early, took Christina Lopez with!"

"I often wondered about her."

"You're raising your voice."

"Am I?"

"Now, your wife! Played Gotcha with her."

"Gotcha?"

"Gotcha once, twice, forty times Gotcha!"

"Wait!"

Walter reared up, clutching his blanket.

"Grab your ears! While you were in Panama, Abbey and I had a wildcat fun-feast!"

"I would have heard."

"Since when do husbands hear? Remember her wine tour in Provence?"

"Right."

"Wrong. She was in Paris drinking champagne from my golf shoes!"

"Golf shoes!?"

"Paris was our nineteenth green! World championships! Then Morocco!"

"She never went!"

"Was there, did that! Rome! Guess who was her tour guide!? Tokyo! Stockholm!"

"Her parents were Swedish!"

"I gave her the Nobel Prize. Brussels, Moscow, Shanghai, Boston, Cairo, Oslo, Denver, Dayton!"

"Stop, oh God, stop! Stop!"

I stopped and, like in old movies, stepped to the window and had a cigarette.

I could hear Walter crying. I turned and saw that he had swung his legs out, letting the tears drip off his nose to the floor.

"You son of a bitch!" he gasped.

"Right."

"Bastard!"

"Indeed."

"Monster!"

"Yes?"

"Best friend! I'll kill you!"

"Catch me first!"

"Then wake and kill you again!"

"What're you doing?"

"Getting outta bed, dammit! Come here!"

"Naw." I opened the door and looked out. "Bye."

"I'll kill you if it takes years!"

"Hey! Listen to him—*years*!"

"If it takes *forever*!"

"Forever! That's rich! Toodle-oo!"

"Freeze, dammit!"

Walter lurched up.

"Son of a bitch!"

"Right!"

"Bastard!"

"Hallelujah! Happy New Year!"

"What!?"

"Prosit! Skoal! What was I once?"

"Friend?"

"Yeah, *friend*!"

I laughed a physician-doctor-medicine man laugh.

"Bitch!" screamed Walter.

"Me, yeah, *me*!"

I jumped out the door and smiled.

"Me!"

The door slammed.

THE COMPLETIST

2003–2004

IT WAS ON A SHIP in the mid-Atlantic in the summer of 1948 that we met the completist—that's what he called himself.

He was a lawyer from Schenectady, well dressed, and he insisted on paying for the drinks when we met by accident before supper, and then made sure that we were seated with him at dinner, rather than at our regular table.

He talked and kept on talking during dinner with wonderful stories, grand jokes, and with an air about him that was convivial and worldly and wise.

At no time did he allow us to speak, and my wife and I were entertained, intrigued, and willing to silence ourselves to let this amusing man describe the world he traveled, from continent to continent, from country to country, and from city to city, collecting books, building libraries, and entertaining his soul.

He told us how he had heard of a fabulous collection in Prague and had spent the better part of a month crossing the world by ship and by train to find and purchase the collection and return it to his vast home in Schenectady.

He had spent time in Paris, Rome, London, and Moscow and had shipped home tens of thousands of rare volumes, which his law practice allowed him to buy.

When he spoke of these things his eyes glowed and his face was suffused with a color that no liquor could induce.

There was no air of braggadocio about this lawyer—he was simply describing, as a cartographer describes a chart—a map of places and events and times he could not help but relate.

While he did all this he did not order any meal that would have to take his attention. He gave little mind to the immense salad before him, which allowed him to keep talking as, on occasion, he devoured a mouthful and then ran on with his descriptions of places and collections all over the world.

Each time my wife and I tried to intrude upon his exclamations, he waved his fork at us and shut his eyes to silence us as his mouth proclaimed yet another wonder.

"Do you know the work of Sir John Soane, the great English architect?" he asked.

Before we could answer he rushed on.

"He rebuilt all of London in his mind and in the drawings made according to his specifications by his artist-friend, Mr. Ginty. Some of his dreams of London were actually built, others were built and destroyed, and yet others remained only figments of his incredible imagination.

"I have found some of his library dreams and worked with the grandsons of his architectural engineers to build on my estate what you would call a steeplechase university. From building to building on this great acreage outside of Schenectady I have placed grand lanterns of education.

"By strolling across my meadows, or better yet—and how romantic—to visit on horseback, from yard to yard, you can find yourself in the grandest library of medical knowledge in the world. I say this because I have found this library in Yorkshire and bought its ten thousand volumes and shipped them home to be safely kept under my hand and eye. Great physicians and surgeons come to visit me and live in the library for days or weeks or months.

"Beyond that, in other locales around my estate, there are small lighthouse libraries of the greatest novels from every country in the world.

"And beyond that, an Italian environment that would have caused Bernard Berenson, the great Italian Renaissance art historian, to go sleepless with envy.

"My estate then, this university, is a series of buildings spread over one hundred acres where you could spend a lifetime without ever leaving my environment.

"On any single weekend, the heads of colleges, universities, and schools in Prague, Florence, Glasgow, and Vancouver collect to enjoy my chef's meals and drink my wines and love my books."

He went on to describe the leather many of the books were bound in, the superb quality of the bindings, the paper used within, and the typefaces.

Beyond that he described how wonderful it was that you could visit his multitudinous centers of learning and walk out in the meadows and seat yourself, to read in an environment that was conducive to vast learning.

"There you almost have it. I'm on my way now to Paris, whence I train south and ship out through the Suez Canal to India, Hong Kong, and Tokyo. Another twenty thousand volumes of art history, philosophy, and world travel await me in these far places. I am like a schoolchild, nervous, awaiting tomorrow, when I will get my hands on these further treasures."

At long last our lawyer friend seemed finished.

The salad was gone, the dessert was finished, and the last of the wine had been drunk.

He gazed into our faces, as if wondering if we had anything to say.

Indeed, there was much we had gathered up and we awaited a chance to speak.

But before we could open our mouths, the lawyer had summoned our waiter again and ordered three double brandies.

My wife and I demurred, but he waved us aside. The brandies were placed before us.

He arose, studied the bill, paid it, and stood for a long while as the color drained from his face.

"There is only one last thing I'd like to know," he said finally.

He shut his eyes for a moment, and when he opened them the light was gone; he seemed to be gazing at a place a million miles off in his imagination.

He picked up his double brandy, held it in his hands, and at last said, "Tell me one last thing."

He paused and then continued.

"Why did my thirty-five-year-old son kill his wife, destroy his daughter, and hang himself?"

He drank the brandy, turned, and without a word, left the ship's dining room.

My wife and I sat there for a long time, eyes shut, and then, without thinking, felt our hands move out and touch the brandy that awaited us.

EPILOGUE:
THE R.B., G.K.C. AND G.B.S. FOREVER ORIENT EXPRESS

1996–1997

And when I die, will this dream truly be
Entrained with Shaw and Chesterton and me?
O, glorious Lord, please make it so
That down along eternity we'll row
Atilted headlong, nattering the way
All mouth, no sleep, and endless be our day:
The Chesterton Night Tour, the Shaw Express,
A picknicking of brains in London dress
As one by one we cleave the railroad steams
To circumnavigate my noon and midnight dreams.
First Shaw arrives and hands me biscuit tin
"Grab on, dear child," he cries. "Get in, get in!"

His voice pure Life Force judge and Mankind's Maker.
G.K. climbs up past Shaw and ticket-taker.
Now down the line trots Dickens, paced by Twain.
"Hold on!" cries Mark. And Dickens: "Stop that train!"
"It's stopped," snorts Shaw, "are your brains packed? Aboard!"
With this last as commandment from our Lord
We jostle up to face each other's wits
As Shaw amidst the mob like statue sits
And maunders up his tongue to launch the Game
His merest cough a shot to walk us lame.
Now Poe arrives in furs, he's dressed for snows
Cold flurries caper him where e'er he goes,
Seen distantly his broad pale brow's a moon
That sinks at daybreak but to rise at noon.
Charles Dickens's stunned, but Twain cries, "Man alive!"
G. Shaw and G.K.? blind, as Deaths arrive
Just I amongst them hear pale Edgar's tune
His pale heartbeat with tone that echoes loon.
Now Wilde wafts on, empurpled are his drums
As something wily-witted this way comes.
And here stalks Melville, Rudyard Kipling too.
Whale's Herman's White, Kim's scribe an Indian hue,
Lord Russell, wily midget, now entrains
His top hat jumbo-size, to cup his brains
And challenge Shaw and Chesterton to chats
While Poe, subsided, scowling, frets their hats
To mend their politics or bend each mind

While steaming Kipling's Country of the Blind.
Ah, hark! Their talk is gold and seldom tin
And boring? Never! God prevent *that* sin!
Muse hone their tongues to razor-sharpened wits
So Shaw can rave while proud Lord Russell sits
And I the modest mouse who locks his lip
And mutters not a mote along the trip,
Most gladly hidden—tucked between these brains
That locomote the night with idea trains,
Each locked to each and each a brighter car
And this a nova, that old Halley's star,
A light-year comet blazed across our sight.
To teach our railway schools throughout our night.
Their philosophic crumbs I snatch and eat,
The hiccoughing of Shaw? my God, a treat!
While Poe grows quieter the more they storm,
His snowy moon brow pale, his tongue lukewarm,
But I am glad for him, for while they range
Poe's eyes with mine do some wry joke exchange,
I see the Black Cat hid where Poe's seams split
His head a Pendulum, his breast a Pit,
While all about our favorite authors drink
In mute Poe's eyes I see dire Usher sink,
Loud Shaw and G.K. take each other to task?
Says Poe: Amontillado? Here's the Casque,
Cap on these bells, while I a mortar mix
To stash these madmen in a cell of bricks.

Thus I in shames, all shambles, keep my peace
As all these angel souls their wings release.
The air is battered by these airborne goats
Who leap and clamber, music in their throats,
Such sweet enchantments! harken to their gab!
Their locomotive thunders shake our cab.
To sound us from the station, what a mix
Of clangor-dins from these most glorious Six.
Their conversation showers me with chat
Till Shaw corks all to point where Truth is at,
Then Chesterton orates the great I Am
Nor shuts for tea and tarts (the last with jam).
And silent midst the rest, now witness Poe.
He dreams himself found dead in winter snow?
While Wilde a beggar starves in Paris keep
And Melville dies on land while critics sleep.
O damn those soul-survivors, why's it so?
That wise men then knew not what we now know?
To tape a Whale but never know its size
And measure Poe but seldom toss him prize?
How laugh at Wilde who now must laugh at you?
I often wonder just what critics do?
I know they read but wonder if they think?
I sip on wine while they the other drink,
But from the selfsame fount, then can it be
The better part of wisdom lies on me?
The books I read they shrug and lob away

To bury until resurrection's day.
What calls these friends from literary tomb?
One voice, one love, one night, one lonely room
Where turning pages I with wild desire
Ran forth to snatch their charred book from the fire?
O dear Poe, never exit; Mr. Wilde
Rise up with Dorian to tease this child
To please this boy again with ghastly tale,
And Herman, tag along with comrade Whale.
I would not spurn you forth or turn you out
Or kill that great White thing with cynic's doubt.
In baggage car waits Dorian, a canvas ghost,
While Wilde at tea bites tongue and lets Shaw boast.
Then Oscar cuts and tosses mot juste
And laughter rings and leaves him in a gust.
The authors bark and yip, their faces shine,
Their vast talk merely beer, while Wilde's is wine.
At last dear Edgar hems and dares to speak,
His Usher voice is winter lost and weak,
His dark heart drums beneath our carriage floor,
The train's smoke ravens by with: Nevermore.
We turn to Melville now and seek his Whale,
What's that? The merest minnow! Drop the sail.
So say the critics, but does Melville hear?
He does and shuns the sea and now his bier.
This midnight train, which rounds the curve ahead,
Its engine ghostly pale, a loom of dread,

Then all's not lost, for whether land or sea,
Old Moby tracks the chase and summons me.
We doubt all this but crowd the pane to spy
That locomoting Whiteness, hear its cry?
With churned Saint Elmo's fires, sweet Christ, what sound!
The sea like God sounds near, we all are drowned.
As down the nightfall path we raving go,
Old Moby dragging us, one train of woe.
"O, bosh!" says Shaw, and sits, to jolt us back,
"That's Industry's Revolt upon the track!"
Much better that than Beast. We sit to eat,
Take tea, a biscuit, bun, or brioche-sweet.
While Kipling curries up remembrance when
His Kim drummed out in dust then back again,
And Kaa was coveted as monarch snake,
And Mowgli howled with wolves that shrilled to shake.
The moon, and pace our train, while our hearts sing:
Aye! Kipling's our Man Who Would Be King!
Then all too soon, the sun burns up at dawn,
No time to cork our sleep or share a yawn,
It's over, for now look, around the bend,
Our final stop! the station where books end.
And authors step and leave and all's good-bye,
I start to think it so and start to cry.
With wicker rustlings now the gods arise,
Their glory burst my chest and cracks my eyes.
The train with muffled heartbeat chuffs to cease,

At Land's End Lost Time Station, hear the peace,
Where just the other breath our life was words,
Now trees are filled with literature of birds.
Shaw jumps down first, with Chesterton close by
And Kipling wipes the tear winks from my eye.
There, funeral of one, comes Mr. Poe
With Melville dressed in white, his face all snow.
Poe grips my hand in silence, does not say
"Farewell" or "Nevermore" but glides away.
While Oscar last of all, now inside sits
To pack and then repack his case of wits,
"This is a special time," he says, "let's try
To say farewells as if we really meant good-bye."
My chin is chucked by Twain, who like the sun
All laughing, buffs my cheek, "God bless you, son."
And there they stroll along the station strand,
With Melville slow and 'lorn and lost on land.
What is this place? a bookshop by the sea?
O, yes! How grand! That fires a joy in me!
They are not lost or dead, for here, next day,
Some other child will travel them away,
On night train journeyings that only slow
At towns where other authors thrive and go
And bark all night and all the glad things know.
Why is this so? Because *I* say it's so.
My friends are gone, I stand a moment more,
To see their footprints sift along the shore,

I wave at shadows, climb aboard my train.
I weep because their likes won't come again.
But this sure thing I know by sounding sea:
Their deaths diminish, words replenish me.
For traveling down the shore in lonely car,
I open wide their books and there they are!